A NOVEL OF NEON BRILLIANCE!

"SUSPENSEFUL...[The authors] unleash two winning characters in the gutsy, determined Egan and the world-weary but all-knowing Kingston...Slick!"

—*Booklist*

"MASTERFUL...The Florida mystery I would unreservedly recommend."

—*Wilson Library Bulletin*

"FAST-PACED...Tantalizing senses, personalities, and imagery."

—*Tri-City Herald (Pasco, WA)*

"A FAST-MOVING MYSTERY whose strengths are the authentic Florida boom-town atmosphere and the Taylors' knowing eye for newspaper detail."

—*Atlanta Journal & Constitution*

"REALISTIC, WELL-WRITTEN AND INTERESTING!"

—*Mystery News*

"Appearances are deceiving...as tension builds."

—*Houston Post*

NEON Flamingo

MATT & BONNIE TAYLOR

SMP

ST. MARTIN'S PAPERBACKS

Published by arrangement with Dodd, Mead

NEON FLAMINGO

Library of Congress Catalog Card Number: 87-15599

ISBN: 0-312-91622-1

Printed in the United States of America

Dodd, Mead hardcover edition published 1987
St. Martin's Paperbacks edition/June 1990

10 9 8 7 6 5 4 3 2 1

To Amy, Patti, John, and George

ONE

You could be forgiven if you'd stumbled on what you thought was a remake of *The Great Gatsby*. There was the huge Spanish building, its pink stucco drenched in Florida sunshine; there was the pale yellow 1935 Packard phaeton; there was the woman, dressed in a crisp white linen skirt and plum blouse; there were the palms and a sniff of salt in the breeze mingling with the woman's scent of gardenias.

But there was also me, so you would have been wrong.

When I saw the white high-heeled shoes against the red brick driveway and heard her voice, louder the second time, I squeezed my big frame out from under the Packard. Oil was smeared on my T-shirt and ragged denim shorts.

"You the landlord?" The question had apprehension in it, as though I wasn't the first one she'd asked.

"I am."

"Have you rented the apartment yet? The little one up high? For two hundred dollars a month?" Her words scurried like fiddler crabs before the surf—nervous, anxious, vulnerable.

She was in her early thirties. A few years behind me, I guessed. Too thin, but not from dieting. It was the way she talked and radiated energy. She'd need fuel like a steam locomotive to keep her fingers dancing on her purse the way they did. Her eyes measured me. No flicker hinted at what she thought about what she was seeing.

"There *is* a place for rent?" she asked again as I grinned at her. "I knew those cops were up to something. Was it all a joke?"

She fumbled with a thin packet of money, carefully arranged and not adding up to much. "I came straight from the police station but I couldn't find you. No answer at your door. I asked your tenants. Five or six of 'em."

"You went banging on my tenants' doors?" From the look on her face, I must have sounded gruff but I was really amused.

"What about the apartment?" She was relentless.

I dragged a dirty arm across my eyes to wipe out the salt. "You're a god-damned reporter, aren't you?" I grumbled. "Going around disturbing my tenants."

Her shoulders drooped. "Damn cops! I knew they were getting their kicks out of me somehow. What is it, you don't rent to reporters? That's against the law, you know."

Her hair was the color of polished coal. It hung straight and short to her jawline, where it curved in all around like an upsidedown poppy blossom, if there's such a thing as a black poppy.

"Mister, I need a place to live. Yes, I'm a reporter. So what? Do you have an apartment for me or not?"

There was no pleading, but I could sense her antsiness. She glanced at the elegant building and I knew she was living in it for that brief moment, trying it on.

2

"It's way up," I said. "There's no elevator and calling it small overstates its size. You better have a look."

"Okay. I'll look, but I'll take it."

I moved ahead of her across the bricks, a Clydesdale leading a ginger-stepping Paso Fino. In the courtyard, I noted that another of this Saturday morning's chores—when I got through with the Packard—would be to clean the green growth out of the crevices in the fountain. Not all of it. Gnarled and old as that fountain is, a little green enhances it.

I led her up the steps and through the cusped archway, to the tiled reception room. "This was originally a tycoon's mansion. Built in the twenties. When the Florida bubble burst, it went for taxes, stood empty for decades, then was converted to apartments in the fifties."

We passed the filigreed iron banisters and columns of the first floor stairs and started up the less ornate second set. By the third stairwell, narrow with only a railing screwed into the wall, I looked back to see how she was faring. Her breathing was as natural and steady as my own.

Unlike the airy fern-lined reception area and the long second-floor corridor with its huge arches on one side, this hall was short and bare and illuminated by only a sixty-five-year-old electric fixture.

"Gotta upgrade here," I mumbled for maybe the fortieth time.

"The hallway's fine," she jumped in. "You can't expect Grand Central Station for two hundred dollars a month." Her fingers danced on her purse and I could imagine her mind calculating where I'd find the money to fix the hall.

"So who you with?" I asked as I fumbled the key into the shiny brass dead bolt I'd installed, one of the few

3

changes I'd made that was out of character with the mansion's style. Old locks could never do the job against today's evils.

"The New Seville *Times*." A glimmering, restrained smile of pride played with her lips.

"That rag," I joked, following her inside. "Well, I can't blame you for living over here in a real city."

She gave me a sharp look.

"This is it," I said. "Living, dining, and kitchen rolled into one. Through that strange little door and down the crooked hallway is the bedroom."

"Oh, I thought it was furnished." She sounded bleak.

"There's a queen-size Sealy, a good, firm one in the bedroom. Go look."

"I could buy a cardtable," she said, walking distractedly through the hallway. I followed closely. I wanted to see her reaction. The room was tiny. But that hadn't mattered to anyone else who'd seen it.

Or to her, it turned out.

She let out a low whistle. Not many women can do that well.

She peered out a wall of giant arched windows at the Florida landscape spread out before us. Floor to ceiling, three wide Spanish windows looked past palms and nearby tile roofs, across the shimmering blue channel to downtown Marlinsport, a half mile away. It was a city of glass high rises, intersecting expressways, and an energy to match her own.

"Yeah. New Seville's got first-rate printing presses and we got the town," I chuckled. It was an old newspaper joke. Plenty of people live across the bay in New Seville, but they're mostly quiet, retired folks, whereas Marlinsport is a working-class town with the working class's lusts and conflicts.

Violet eyes narrowed and darted over my sun-weathered face. She didn't seem to like my joke, but then I really didn't expect her to, her being filled with a newcomer's zeal for a job.

"That door at the end of the hall outside goes into the attic. There's a lot of wicker and cane stuff in there. You're welcome to what you like."

"At the same rate," she murmured.

"Same rate."

Her fingers stopped their dancing. She stood captivated by the view. "It's a great place," she said after a minute. "I can't believe it's mine."

Her relief and honesty touched me. I told her yes, it was hers and led her back to the front room to show her how the stove worked.

When she squatted down beside me to peer into the oven, I turned, my face inches from her own, and asked, "What's your name?"

"Alice Jane Egan," she replied as we both stood back up. "I go by A.J. And I guess I ought to be getting back over to the police station."

"Want to sign a lease and get a key first?"

"Oh, yeah." A finger moved once more on her purse.

Back down stairs we walked silently toward my apartment on the first floor. As she waited in the doorway I filled out the short form.

"What shift has the *Times* got you working?" I asked, just to make conversation.

"Marlinsport cop shop five days." Again there was a hint of pride around those straight lips. "Nights Monday,

Tuesday, and Friday, and weekends."

"Doesn't sound like a very good schedule."

She grinned. "Maybe not, but it's a great chance for me. I came here from a small paper in the middle of Kansas and right off the bat I get to go up against Palmer Kingston."

"He's with the Marlinsport *Tribune*, right?"

"Yeah, but he's about the only thing that sheet has going for it."

Something in her countenance when she said that made me wonder if she didn't think the right woman might knock that bird right off his perch.

"The *Trib*'s served this town pretty well for ninety years," I offered.

Her violet eyes opened innocently "Oh? Is that the age of their presses? I hear they have to kick the damn things to get them started."

Her words were close to the truth and no put-down by me of the *Times* would change that. I was saved the necessity of thinking up a reply by the ringing of my phone. I excused myself, answered it, talked for maybe two minutes, then rejoined her.

"I gotta go," I said and scrawled my name on the lease. I was rooting around for the right key when her purse began to beep like a geiger counter. She extracted a pager and stilled it.

"The city desk," she said. "Can I use your phone?"

"Okay, but hurry," I said, even though it wasn't necessary. I knew what her call would be.

She punched through to her editor and in moments was making notes on the margin of her copy of the lease. At the same time it looked like she was studying my signature. It was hard to tell which interested her more, what she was writing or what she was reading. When she hung up, she held out the lease to me, a slender, clear-polished nail pointing to my name.

"It's messy but that looks like it could be J. P. Kingston there," she said.

"Everybody calls me Palmer."

She tucked the paper and pager into her purse and her purse under her arm. "I don't guess either of us has time to talk now," she said, "but maybe one day you can tell me how a career reporter manages to get all this . . ." Her gesture took in the building, the yard, the car. I laughed feebly. I needed to get going.

"If you're gonna be a career reporter, you better have something like this," I said. "S'cuse me. I've got to change clothes."

She edged out the door.

I watched her run tip-tapping through the brick circle past the fountain and the Packard and out to the road, where she'd parked her car, a little red VW Beetle, one of those convertibles with a top that folds back like a rickshaw. She turned it around in the middle of the street and sped off like she knew where she was going. I could imagine her poring over a Marlinsport map back in Kansas waiting to start this job. And I wondered if for once the *Times* might have hired somebody who'd ask hard questions instead of coasting through life on an Ivy League diploma.

But this was not the time for journalistic or competitive reflection. I needed to get out to Haskins Delano's house where I had every reason to expect I'd see A.J. Egan again. On the way I could puzzle over the irony of a thirty-year cop like Delano being murdered at home a year and a half after retiring from the force.

TWO

The shady street in Hyde Park was about as I expected—crowded. I parked near the corner and walked past a number of police cars, along with a couple bearing *Trib* parking stickers, A.J.'s little Bug, the mobile crime lab, the medical examiner's wagon, and the police chief's chrome and black Chrysler. Television vans blocked the sidewalks, the camera crews in ragged clothes providing live coverage of overdressed reporters who were projecting not much information but lots of emotion.

Weaving my way through the equipment and cars, I felt a bit emotional myself. Death chills the air, even on a humid morning in Florida. And Delano had played a big part in my life.

His two-story house was blue-shingled. Around it were the ostentatiously restored homes of lawyers and bankers, with catered lawn services and rich new brasswork. Delano's was just old. It was kept up, but not lavishly. He'd tried to get a coat of paint to do the work of new lumber. There are a lot of neighborhoods like it in Marlinsport.

A couple of cops nodded me past the yellow and black crime-scene tape. I climbed the three concrete steps with the inevitable crack in them. The screen door was jammed open, the front door stood ajar. On the porch A.J. was quizzing the chief of detectives, and the *Trib*'s weekend police reporter, Randy Holliman, was taking notes.

I squeezed into the crowded living room, staying out of the way and trying to be inconspicuous, a real coup if I could pull it off.

" 'Lo, Palmer."

" 'Lo, Chief. Harry. Benny ."

Poor old Delano was a god-awful mess. The air was filled with the tangy smell of his blood despite the open door. His body was hunched forward in a stuffed chair, its yellow and green slipcover stained red, turning blackish brown. Puddles of blood spread out around Delano's bare feet. The back of his sweatshirt was slashed in a dozen places. The medical examiner eased Delano back, briefly, and showed me the streams of blood from several abdominal wounds. The bunched waistband of boxer shorts peeked out the top of stained sweatpants.

The room had been gone through hastily, drawers were pulled and a desk ransacked. An open jar of paste was on the table beside Delano's chair. Newspaper was scattered across the floor.

"Same in the bedroom," Chief Emilio Salgado said as he caught my wandering eye. "Drawers, pictures, books tossed around."

He gripped my arm hard. I tilted an ear to catch the menace in his Spanish-tinged promise. "Don't be around when we catch this one, Palmer."

I grunted sympathetically. "You got any idea what it's all about?"

The little chief rocked on his heels. "Not yet. But this crime has a history. So we'll get him. And when we do, I'll grind him into *boliche*."

If not in size, at least by force of presence, Chief Salgado dominated the room. He's a good old cop who busted his pick cleaning up the more violent aspects of gambling and corruption in Marlinsport. And if the force isn't squeaky clean—and no police force that I know of is—it's not from a lack of scrubbing on his part.

"What do you mean history?" I asked him. "You think Escobar's people had anything to do with this?"

"No, the mob doesn't kill in a frenzy. This is the work of someone Delano caught, or caused trouble for."

"Look at this, Chief," Benny, kneeling, called from across the room. Amid the papers on the floor was a print in blood of the bottom of a sneaker; man's, medium size, I'd guess.

"Good job," Salgado said. "Be careful with it. That old *Trib* might put a cop killer in the chair."

As I left the house later, I saw that A.J. had captured an assistant state attorney. He seemed a willing prisoner.

It was getting toward noon. I shaded my eyes and glanced at the neighborhood. As I said, mostly brass lights and leaded glass. But across the street there was one house with a screened porch that was as neat and unpretentious as Delano's. If he had friendly relations with any of his neighbors, the people in that house would be the ones.

I didn't walk straight over but drifted north a bit, then crossed to the other side and plodded south. There were two elderly women seated opposite each other in matching white swings, and in the shadows on the screen porch I could see a tall old man leaning against the doorjamb.

"Morning," I said, letting the natural Cracker in my voice drawl out more than usual.

A trio of voices repeated the word, not quite in unison. I nodded back toward Delano's house.

"It's terrible, isn't it?"

A chorus of "Terrible, terrible" floated out to me. Across the street we could see a couple of neighbors lining up for interviews before a TV camera.

"Ha!" one of the women exclaimed. "They won't get nothing from that pair. Hardly gave Haskins the time of day."

"You knew Captain Delano?" I asked.

"You one of those TV men?" she asked right back.

"No. My name's Palmer Kingston." I squinted in the sun. "I'm with the *Trib*."

"I know you," the old man coughed. Ignoring him, the woman stretched out to crack open the screen door.

"Come sit by me," she said. "It's too hot to stand out there."

She shifted her weight to one side of the porch swing and I did as I was told. She was soft to look at but it was laid in over a steel skeleton. She had a pasty white face, rimless glasses, white hair piled in a knot on top of her head, and wattles trembling from her pink chin.

"I'm Louella Ragsdale. This is my sister, Zelda Thornberg, and he's her husband. Would you like something to drink?" she asked as I sat down.

"It is a warm one," I ventured. "Thanks."

"Carl, why don't you get Mr. Kingston a drink." It was more a command than a request. She smiled at me. "You been in the house. Who did it?"

I spoke easily but with care.

"They don't know . . . yet."

"And him a policeman."

Carl reappeared holding a glass.

"Well, for heaven's sake, why'd you bring tap water? Get the sun tea off the back porch and I'll have one, too."

Poor Carl, rawboned, big-eared, and not overly bright, wouldn't surrender.

"Just before this fellow walked up you said the tea wouldn't be ready for a while. You said that."

"Carl, that was a half hour ago. My, your mind does wander."

She turned her understanding smile on me. "Carl and Zelda have lived with me ever since his retirement."

"Not at first we didn't," the bony old man interjected. "We did fine at first." He clamped his jaw shut, pondering his life.

"Now you've already forgotten the tea, Carl, honey." Her patter was like being spanked with a saturated powder puff.

I asked then about Delano, half in an attempt to get her to forget the tea.

"Well, I can't believe his ex-wife did it," she began.

"No," I agreed.

"Even if he was mean to her . . . when was it Marjorie moved out, Zelda?"

"Before our time," her sister answered.

"Oh, well, let me see . . . . He retired a couple of years ago and she left him a number of years before that."

Muttering to himself, Carl banged his way back onto the porch with a huge pitcher and four glasses on a tray. I lost Louella's attention.

"Where's the ice, Carl, honey? And the sugar?"

"I'll get them," Zelda said, scurrying into the house.

"I damned near got a hernia bringing this out," Carl observed.

Louella ignored his remark and raised her voice to a genteel shout aimed toward the interior of the house. "Don't forget spoons! Carl must think Mr. Kingston stirs his tea with his fingers."

Finally the logistics of the iced tea were worked out to Louella's satisfaction.

"Did you know her?" I asked.

"Marjorie? She sat in this swing every day for as long as she lived in that house. But she had little to say about him. They were very different. God knows why they got married."

"After she left, did he have women in?" I kept it low and intimate. I didn't think it was the kind of topic elderly women would discuss in a normal tone.

"Haskins Delano! Have a woman in!" Louella let out a shriek that set a cameraman across the street fumbling with his sound equipment.

"Lord, what for?" she scoffed. "He was an old man. What would any woman want with him?" Her laugh seemed to cut Carl, but for once he didn't raise an argument.

"What did Delano do with himself after his retirement?"

"He had a garden."

Louella ruminated for a moment, then her eye settled on Carl. "You might look back there this afternoon," she told him. "No reason to let good tomatoes rot on the vine."

She turned back to me. "Give the devil his due;

Haskins could make anything grow. The only thing he ever did well . . . Of course, he may have been a perfectly good policeman."

"Of course," I agreed quickly. "I knew Delano but I haven't seen him since he got his captaincy and retired."

Louella leaned toward me in a conspiratorial way. "He had some bitterness about his work, you know. Although that was a minor refrain compared to his feelings for the press."

Before I could ask her what she meant, Carl slapped his hands in the air like he was killing a mosquito. "Whooie! Hask hated the press. God, he did that," he cackled. "Hey, I know where I've heard of you."

Grinning broadly, he pointed at me. "Hask had a whole scrapbook full of your stories. He didn't like you at all."

"Carl, sit down."

"Wait a minute. Delano had something against me? What?"

"He never said, but way back somewhere you did something that ticked him off good. Every time your name showed up on a story he'd stew over it."

My surprise tickled Carl. "I ought to know," he said. "I sometimes walked with Hask to Five Points at night to get the papers."

Louella snorted. "I thought the papers were incidental to the trip to the bar."

"We stopped by the bar so Hask could lay the papers out side by side," Carl spluttered. "If the headlines weren't the same, he'd holler that one or the other paper didn't know what it was doing. Then when he got home he'd cut and swear and fill those scrapbooks."

"Now, Carl, don't excite yourself," Louella soothed.

But the old man was on a roll. "Makes me wonder what old Hask would think about having his body found by the paperboy."

"How'd you find out about that?" I asked.

"The cops weren't exactly quiet when they got here," he snickered. "Half the neighborhood was standing on Hask's front lawn by ten. So the cops told us a little to get us to go home."

"It was rough on you, I know, losing a friend."

"I played dominoes with him. That's all," Carl said stubbornly.

"Of course, we're all upset about his murder," Louella put in. "Poor Zelda's scared out of her mind it'll happen to us."

I turned to the smaller woman. "The police will keep a watch on the street until this is settled."

I could tell by the tremor in her hands that my words did not reassure her and I was about to try again when my attention was diverted across the street. Salgado was emerging from Delano's house. Knowing he was not one for long good-byes, I extricated myself and hurried to the chief's car. His driver had the Chrysler cranked up, and icy air blew on my face as the electric window on the chief's door slid down.

"You find a scrapbook anywhere in Delano's?" I asked.

The chief and his driver exchanged glances.

"Scrapbook," the chief repeated. Then, hard at me, "Off the record?"

"For now, yes."

"There was a big gap in his bookcase where several large books would go. Dust marks outlined them. But there's no books like that in the house. Did Delano keep scrapbooks?"

"Hated the press," I said.

The chief's eyes said what else was new.

"More than ordinary. He'd go buy the bulldog editions to compare at night, then get the morning *Trib* delivered, too."

"That explains the stack of old clipped papers on the back porch," the chief said.

I could see Salgado's mind working as the window rolled up and his driver inched the car into the street.

I was on my way back into Delano's to poke around a bit, maybe get a look at those papers, but young, stocky Randy Holliman motioned to me. He was carrying a portable radio on his belt. I'm supposed to carry one, too, but I don't.

"The desk has called three times for you. Wilson must be pissed. Wants to see you—now."

Our boss. The latest managing editor. If he was mad at me, it was no novelty.

I grumbled, but told Randy to radio the desk that I was coming in.

As I walked back up the narrow street, I saw A.J. Egan rapping on the door of Delano's next-door neighbor.

THREE

Since it was Saturday and the *Tribune*'s front doors were locked, I flipped my ID card for the guard at the back stairs and climbed up to the newsroom. As the stairway door closed behind me, I heard Smitty below speaking my name into the radio. I had a pretty good idea it was the city desk that wanted to be tipped when I got in.

I was right. Not just beads but puddles of sweat formed on Moses Johnson's ribbed, bald head as he ran to meet me in the hall. His adam's apple worked in the loose red skin of his neck. A city editor running is like a pope playing volleyball. There is no way to do it right. It offends the eye.

But at fifty Moses was overstressed, fighting for survival, and losing. Three years ago the Marlinsport *Tribune* was bought by a newspaper chain, and chains want young, cheap editors, not packed retirement rolls. An outsider, Robert Wilson, was the latest installed as managing editor to give the chain what it wanted.

"The old man's upset with you," Moses began.

"The old man? You mean Wilson? Hell, he's barely in his thirties."

"You should have called in."

I kept walking at a good clip down the hall. We passed composing, then photo.

"What's Wilson's problem?"

Moses was anguished. I figured he must have been catching hell all morning on my account.

"He wants to know what's going on. And, damn it, I should know!"

"You sent me to Delano's. You knew I'd get the story."

At the newsroom door I stopped. In a glance I took it all in. Why Moses was so tied up in knots. Across the large room with its skeleton weekend crew, through his glass walls, I saw Robert Wilson's council of war—Scott Brown, the news editor, and red-haired Paula Prince, hired by Wilson to assist the unlucky Moses. She was half his age and untroubled by self-doubt.

Paula's fierce eyes glittered when she caught sight of me. I saw her mouth the words "Here he is" as she waved me toward the closed-door session.

Moses was hanging back. I grabbed him by the elbow and propelled him ahead of me toward Wilson's door.

With an unconscious deference to me, Paula moved from one of the blue chairs by Wilson's desk to the couch. Scott, in the other chair, nodded his dark face noncommittally. Wilson's first words were for Moses.

"Now that you've found your staff, will you make sure the weekly club news is in-house?"

What he meant was for Moses to get the hell out. The beleaguered city editor had such little self-confidence remaining that he actually smiled at us before he left.

18

"Close the door," Wilson called after him.

The door clicked quietly and Wilson turned on me. His hazel eyes narrowed in a frown, by now an expression everyone in the newsroom knew well.

"Don't you know to keep in touch with the goddamned desk when you're on a big story?"

I looked to Paula. "Have you changed my work schedule?"

She started to shake her Irish red hair, caught herself, and said, "Don't start that kinda shit, Palmer. You know what he means."

It was bad form on my part. No real reporter or line editor can worry about a forty-hour week. But I was not about to roll over for Wilson.

"I am working this story on my own time and had to break it off, it seems, to come in just to get my ass chewed. You don't get to do that."

"You let me worry about what I can and can't do. I haven't got time for a jousting match over comp time. Take what you've got coming, but do it after this story's done."

I didn't rise to the bait. We both knew he'd deliberately misstated my remark to serve his own purposes. But that's one way he became an editor on the rise at age thirty-two. I'd seen the game too many times to want to play it with him.

Instead I turned to Scott Brown. "You gonna lead with it?"

"Of course we're going to lead with it." Wilson jumped back in. "The only question is how big we should go."

So that's what I was here for. Not a stick of type in the house yet and our bright managing editor was laying out the front page. But he needed somebody who really knew the town to make sure he and Paula did it right and didn't make fools of themselves.

It was time for me to earn my money. I sucked in two liters of air and let it out slowly.

"Haskins Delano was a hard-luck cop," I began, "not very smart, not very likable, not at all kind."

Over my left shoulder Paula called from the couch. "Was he on the take?"

I shifted uneasily. Editors always ask that question first; it makes them seem smart and tough. "I don't think so," I said. "But there was a . . . malicious undercurrent at the station about him, going back even before I knew him."

"I thought you were here for the Creation," Wilson interjected.

I smiled. "No, I didn't get here until they bit the apple."

"A more likely motive is revenge," Paula said.

Wilson looked at her approvingly.

"Delano wasn't very effective. He took forever to make lieutenant and had to be phonied up for captain," I said.

"We got a dead nobody?" Scott muttered in his usual low monotone.

"Bullshit," said Wilson.

"A dead police captain's a dead police captain," Paula pronounced.

I let them finish.

"If revenge was the motive, maybe we ought to look around here," I said. "Delano didn't have the usual cop's distaste for the press. He loathed us. Maybe he got under some reporter's skin."

"Well, for Christ's sake, we're not putting that in the paper," Wilson shouted. "What kind of cop was he anyway?"

"A loner. The closest Delano came to a friend at the station was the chief," I said. "Salgado was hardly his champion, but he covered for him, got Delano his promotions."

"Why?" Wilson asked.

"Dunno. Loyalty, maybe. Delano was dependable."

"Fuck loyalty," Wilson said. "He had something on the chief."

"Yeah," from the couch.

"What happened this morning?" Scott cocked his long, narrow head to get my full profile.

"You've heard the basic stuff from Randy, right?" I asked. "News carrier came to collect—"

"One of ours," Wilson interrupted. "Circulation manager brought him up here. Kid was scared shitless."

"Randy says there's speculation Delano may have been out jogging, ran into the would-be killer, and brought him home for some reason," Paula said.

"Delano hadn't been jogging," I said.

"Well, we're working on a neighborhood map with the art department," Paula insisted. "Randy's located a man on the next street who thinks Delano jogs past his house every morning about six. Wouldn't that time fit in with the medical examiner's estimate?"

"Yeah."

"And I've got black-and-white art coming in of a pair of worn jogging shoes upstairs beside Delano's bed."

Wilson appeared convinced.

"That must be it," he agreed. I could see he was liking the story more and more. "We could damn near do a minute-by-minute chronology of the last hour of his life. A team of reporters could . . ."

I held up a hand. "Delano was an overweight, overage,

tomato-growing ex-cop who wore sweatpants over boxer shorts. Either of you guys ever wear boxer shorts to go jogging?"

Wilson's eyes met mine, then darted over to Paula's. I heard her sigh.

"So much for that theory," she said. "I'll call off the hounds."

She didn't make any move to leave the room, though. Paula wasn't about to miss any of this.

"Not robbery, surely," Scott said tentatively.

"Off the record . . ." I began.

"Oh, shit, Palmer, you haven't tied us up with some goddamn deal, have you?" Wilson demanded.

Paula groaned. Scott uncrossed his legs like he'd be out the door if the chance arose.

"You want to know or don't you?" I asked evenly.

"I don't want to know anything the city desk's already got—or can get," Paula declared.

"The *Trib*'s not going to be held hostage to some Cracker cop because you decided to take the easy road." Wilson drew himself up and thrust his square chin toward me with indignation.

I looked at him coolly.

"Okay," I said. "Everybody struck their pose now?"

I waited.

At last Wilson broke. "Cut the fucking sarcasm and give us what you got."

I ticked off the points on my fingers.

"First, I've made no deals. What I'm saying is off the record because it needs to be.

"Second, Salgado is Hispanic. Calling a Latin a Cracker reveals a deep ignorance about the community this paper covers.

22

"Third, Moses and I are probably the only Crackers left in the newsroom, and fourth, only Crackers get to call Crackers Crackers without it being an insult."

"Stuff it, Palmer."

"Fifth, here's what happened at Delano's."

"Well, at last."

"Unhunh. Delano was probably asleep upstairs. There was a knock at the door."

"How do you know that?" Paula demanded.

"The doorbell's broken."

"Maybe he heard someone breaking in," she suggested.

"Good catch, Paula," Wilson said, pointing at her.

"Negative," I said. "There's no evidence of forced entry. More to the point, Delano's fully loaded revolver was on the floor under the head of his bed. If he'd been alarmed, he would have carried it downstairs."

"Right," Paula said distinctly, caring more for the truth than pretense. I like that about her.

"That also helps confirm the estimated time of death—about eight-thirty this morning."

"What does one thing have to do with the other?" the news editor asked. He'd never been a reporter and his question showed it.

"Delano was not an early riser. The police figure he was still upstairs at eight or so when the knock came. Any earlier and he might have hauled that revolver with him."

Paula raced ahead. "So the killer confronts Delano, stabs him, ransacks the house, and mutilates the body in a frenzy—maybe frustration at not finding whatever he's looking for . . . What was he looking for, Palmer?"

"They don't know. That's what's off the record."

"I don't follow."

"Obviously whatever he was hunting for is a key to the

23

killer's identity. But they do know what he took and they don't want the killer to know they know."

"What's that?" Wilson rumbled.

"Off the record," I repeated, "scrapbooks. Delano's memorabilia of the things he loved to hate—newspapers in general, me in particular."

"You?" Wilson seemed to like that.

"Yeah. I was apparently number one on his hate list. And I don't have the vaguest idea why."

"So we forget the scrapbooks for now," Paula said.

I nodded.

"I've got something else," Wilson said.

"Yeah?"

"Yeah," he mocked me. "I haven't been off the streets that long. The carrier told me that Delano was still alive when he got to the door."

"Not possible," I said.

"Okay," Wilson replied, "but the kid thought he was alive."

"Why?"

"He saw the door ajar and called out. There was no answer, but when the kid stepped inside and saw Delano slumped over in a puddle of blood, he heard breathing."

"Holy Jesus Christ," I muttered.

"Right," Wilson agreed. "Delano's attacker was still in the room. It's a damn good thing the kid went next door to call the police, giving the killer a chance to slip out the back."

Reality, as it will do, had crept into the newsroom and iced our spines. In our minds, the four of us backed down Delano's steps with that newspaper boy, urging him to run.

Wilson stood. It was a signal of dismissal and decision that Paula and Scott recognized. They stood, too.

24

"We'll lead with it," Wilson ordered tersely, "but use restraint. And I want to see the art." He turned from Scott and Paula to me, still seated in his blue chair. "Dump all your notes on Randy. He'll do the main story."

I nodded.

"Un-ass the furniture, Palmer. It's time for you to show why you're still drawing a paycheck. I want a sidebar from you good enough for page one."

"That says what?"

"Take the long view of Delano's career. See if we can include in tomorrow's paper whatever cost him his life. You know the drill."

Scott and Paula left quickly. I arose slowly and crossed to the doorway.

"Palmer."

Wilson was not very tall but even in Saturday sports clothes instead of a blue-striped suit he looked like a man accustomed to command.

"Unhunh."

"I know you were the razzle-dazzle crime reporter on the old *Trib*, but in the nine months I've been here you've had a byline in the fucking paper twelve times. We're paying you more per word than Hemingway ever got."

Before I could reply, he abruptly changed his manner toward me. His voice dropped and seemed almost confiding. "Your sidebar could be nothing, I know. But if you bring it off . . . if we can include a hint of what turns out to be the motive . . . now that's newspapering."

I had the decency to allow him his honest moment. Then silently, without expression, I left his office and headed for the library.

FOUR

The librarian ran me off copies of the clips that mentioned Delano. The pile was small but most cops don't get their names in the newspaper much. I only scanned a few headlines. The session with Wilson had cost valuable time and I'd be playing catch-up the rest of the day. The clips would keep until later.

Grabbing a city directory, I found Marjorie Delano's address and soon was on my way. Big, dark clouds were forming over the bay. I regretted driving the Packard instead of my old Jeep. Putting up the top would be no ordeal but I don't ever like to drive it in bad weather. Too risky.

Delano's ex-wife lived in Sunset Park, not far from his house but not nearly as interesting an area. The bungalows and apartments reflected the dull stamp of post–World War II construction.

As I turned down her street, there was a surprise for me. Pulling away from the curb was a fire-engine-red VW convertible. A.J. Egan obviously hadn't had to waste time spoon-feeding the ego of her editors.

I was probably going to have to work at convincing Marjorie Delano to see another reporter. I took A.J.'s spot in front of the modest duplex and, grumbling, took the time to put up the Packard's canvas. The sidewalk split to doors on both sides of a screened porch. I rang the bell bearing Mrs. Delano's name. The sound of high heels on tile steps let me know hers was the upper unit.

Her dark eyes were intelligent and leery. Her close-cut, feathered hair had a strong chestnut tinge.

"I've already told that woman reporter everything," she insisted. "Can't you get your story from her?"

"No. But I'll try to make it as easy on you as I can."

She was wearing a crisp print sundress with wide blue shoulder straps and a modestly cut neckline. I considered somberly how differently she and Delano had aged. Here she was in a cheerful costume with a smile on her face, and there he'd been in that dark old house.

"Don't overdo the sympathy routine," she said. "I'm sorry he died the way he did. But don't treat me like the delicate grieving widow. I don't need it and I'm not going to play the role. Come on up."

Poor Delano hadn't exactly overwhelmed people with his passing.

Clattering up and down stairs hadn't hurt her, I thought as I followed. Her body was tight, slender, and graceful in its quickness; something altogether pleasant to contemplate from the rear.

Upstairs she pointed me to a chair, sat on a soft beige sofa, and waited.

"I knew Captain Delano from the squad room," I

started, "and he was involved in my first big story."

"Do you know he detested you?" she asked, giving me an appraiser's look.

"I'm finding that out," I said. "I don't know why."

It was a question she chose to ignore. I tried another. "Did you see him much, in the last years, I mean?"

"Oh, I went over to the house now and then, mostly when I thought he was out, but I always took a friend with me," she said casually. "I've got belongings stored there."

She read my face.

"No, I didn't trust him. He beat me once, badly. I started to file charges but he pleaded with me not to, said the press would destroy him. So I didn't, but I left."

"Why didn't you kick him out?"

"I didn't want that crummy old place. It's mine now but I'll sell it as soon as I can."

"You think your ex-husband could have been killed by a woman he was mistreating?" I asked.

Her reply was quick. "I was the only woman, ever, in Hask's life, and that was a mistake for him as well as me."

"How'd you meet him?"

"Ever hear of the Casino?"

"Ahh. In Alverez District."

"I was a dancer there."

"You have a dancer's body."

Her eyes twinkled with pleasure. "It was the best show in town," she said proudly.

"With one of the best bolita games in back."

Her dark, chiseled eyebrows shot up. "You did know the Casino."

"I've heard of people who bet a dollar or two on the balls when it got too hot to dance. Did Delano?"

She laughed. "I doubt it. Hask was a penny-pincher."

28

"So what was he doing there?"

"Hask was detailed to the Casino one night a week, to give the old police chief, MacDonald, a presence."

"But Delano wasn't on the take?"

She fixed her dark eyes on me. "You don't beat around the bush, do you? No, Hask tried to be an honest cop. That might be what drew me to him in the first place. The only thing I ever saw him take was a meal. He said he couldn't leave the Casino but he couldn't afford the Casino's prices. He loved the pompano en papillote. He never took money."

"Just the fish."

"Look," she laughed, "there were plenty of newsmen back then who didn't mind a free meal. Anyway, on his nights off Hask started coming in. Finally he asked me out and I've got to tell you he was really good-looking in those years." She shook her head sadly. "I mistook him for the strong, silent type—you know, the Bogart image. I didn't see his nasty side until after the honeymoon. It got worse after the raid."

"What raid?"

"Our righteous governor sent in the state police, but it was a set-up. The usual customers, the political powers in Marlinsport, weren't there. Neither were the owners."

I knew what was coming.

"Only the hired help, a few dancers, and a moonstruck cop got arrested. The press—even the guys who were regulars there—tore us up."

I shifted uncomfortably. "Mrs. Delano, I was in John Gorrie Elementary School when that raid took place."

"Well, it was a smear job," she said. "The arrest was on page one, but when the charges were dropped we couldn't even get a story on the same page as the truss ads."

"That doesn't happen anymore," I said halfheartedly.

She leaned back in her chair. "That didn't help Delano. He was the butt of every cop joke in town."

There was an awkward silence between us.

"He made me quit dancing." She was picking her words carefully, I knew. "I stayed home for years but Hask never got over it. Finally I began to sneak out dancing when he was on night duty, and when he found out, well, that's when I left him." A smile unexpectedly softened her face. "Oh, don't look so stricken, Mr. Kingston. It would have happened sooner or later anyway. Still, I'm sorry he came to such a cruel death. No one deserves that."

"Chief Salgado thinks his murder may be tied to an old case," I said. "What do you think?"

She reflected a moment or two, then brushed away whatever images there were.

"Hask was not a talker. If he was afraid of anyone he never told me. As you know, for many years he worked a desk."

She must have sensed my disappointment because her eyes seemed almost mocking as she said, "Well, there was that case involving your own paper. The kidnapping of the publisher's grandson."

"That's when I first met your . . . husband."

"You don't need to tell me that, Palmer Kingston."

"Is that when he got so mad at me? God, Mrs. Delano, I was barely more than a boy."

"It's really odd, talking to you about this. Hask's dead and you're the one sent to interview me about him. If the dumb flatfoot could come back he'd strangle us both."

"Aren't you going to tell me what angered him so?"

She shook her head. "If you really care, dig out your old stories on the kidnapping. The answer's there. It's a trifle but it's there."

"Thanks," I said, and rose to go. "I really do want to know."

"One more thing," she said, following me down the stairs, "Hask became belligerent and drank a lot in later years. Maybe he insulted a drinking crony one time too many."

"Maybe."

The day's heat was broken. I'd spent a lot more time with Marjorie Delano than I'd intended.

"Thanks for talking to me," I said.

"Try not to be too hard on old Hask. Or me," she replied.

On the back of one of the *Trib*'s business cards I carefully printed my home address and pressed it into her hand.

"There's a party tonight, late, at my place. Dancing to live music. Come if you can."

She turned the card. There was a playful sparkle in her eyes.

"Well, your timing is kind of bad, but what the hell. It's the first party invitation Hask ever got me. I just might show up."

I dashed to the Packard as fat drops of rain began.

"Mrs. Delano," I called. "Do come. I've got something you'll really want to see."

FIVE

Tiny wipers slashed at the windshield as the Packard's fat tires sizzled on the downtown streets. Humid air inside the car fogged all the windows and I had to use my handkerchief to swab a patch to see through. Surrounded by Marlinsport's new glass skyscrapers, all cool and plush inside, I fancied in my more elemental environment that I was steaming past out of another era. In the blurred lights I saw the streets as they were two decades ago when both Delano and I were pulled into the kidnapping drama.

In the seedy twilight of the executive offices I had sat apprehensive and perplexed, listening to the murmur of voices from Peter Chastain's office. I was alone on a battered wooden bench with a spindle back. Antiques suited the *Trib* in those days. We were still in the pieced-together buildings downtown, appreciated only by the mice and roaches.

I heard Archie Lameroux mention my name.

"Which one is he?" Chastain growled anxiously.

"That tall, willowy lad" came the answer from the *Trib's* editor-in-chief.

"Scrawny. I've seen him. He'll do," said a voice I didn't recognize.

The rest of the conversation was low-keyed and hard to follow. At times it seemed like bickering over money.

I was green but I wasn't stupid. Something big was afoot. Inside were a number of *Tribune* executives, including the comptroller, Walter Hammersmith. I'd also spied the police chief and several FBI agents.

Familiar faces hurried past me in and out of the sanctum. The hollow-eyed classified ad manager slunk through. I heard him speak a few words about his deadline and then a string of yesses after Chastain ordered, "Get it in. The first item in 'Personals.' "

The ad manager loped out of there like a farmer crossing two furrows at a time.

The old bench creaked under my weight, negligible though it was back then. I was only nineteen, but beginning my second year as a full-time paid staffer. I'd been a sports stringer all through high school and for years it was a joke around the *Trib* that I was going to J school in the fall. The closest I ever came was a few history classes at Marlinsport University.

Hammersmith's assistant, carrying a briefcase, was the next to show up. He went in without knocking and the *Trib* security guard who'd followed him sat down beside me.

"What's happening?" he whispered.

To my shrug he spit out, "Reporters!" and shifted violently on the bench.

I glanced in the office door, not completely closed by the last arrival, and I recognized the president of the largest bank in town talking to Chastain, who was seated at a desk before an open suitcase full of money. Archie Lameroux caught sight of me and closed the door.

There was the feeling of undisturbed dust suspended above me on the old light fixtures and copings. From the inner office came the clatter of a typewriter, followed by judicious murmuring. It was fifteen minutes more before Lameroux's gaunt figure appeared at the doorway. He thrust an envelope toward me, pulled a notebook from his jacket, and read to me these instructions: "Take this envelope to the telephone booth opposite Gate J at Union Station and wait for a call. If you get one, follow the caller's instructions exactly, as though they came from me."

"Sir?" I was acutely aware of how stupid I sounded, but I couldn't help myself.

Lameroux was not sympathetic. "Are my instructions not clear? Shall I repeat them?"

"No, sir. I understand. Answer the phone."

"If the caller asks who you are, tell him and say you are acting for Peter Chastain."

"Yes, sir," I said, my eyes dropping to the envelope in my hand.

"You will not open that unless your caller instructs you to do so," he said. "Now hurry on over there, son—and do your best."

My long, thin legs took me quickly down the worn granite staircase to the second floor. Risking the wrath of Lameroux, and even Chastain himself, I dashed into the classified phone room with its cracked green plaster walls and hot lights hanging by long cords and eased my way to Betsy Fisher's cubicle.

"I'm going to be late," I whispered, bending over her desk like a daddy longlegs. She looked up. Disappointment was in her cobalt eyes.

34

"I'm working," I mumbled, and then was out the door and down the stairs. As soon as I hit the pavement I broke into a run to make up for the minute I'd stolen with Betsy.

Union Station, with its high, vaulted ceiling, was a cavernous echo chamber. But even in those days it was approaching the end of its life as a transportation center. As a child, I had thought it the starting point of romance, where steam engines and Pullmans hissed and groaned. By the time I was a reporter only a few diesels a day carried the handful of passengers who still traveled by rail. By Gate J was a coffee counter. I ordered a cup and settled in. There were not many people in the terminal, and none of them looked interested in me. I was on my second cup of coffee when the phone rang.

It was Archie Lameroux.

"You have not yet received your call."

"No, sir."

"Continue your vigil. We shall discuss later your dalliance in the classified phone room."

I croaked out a "Yes, sir" and returned to my tepid coffee.

The phone rang again.

I dashed to it. But there was no one on the line. After a few more minutes it rang again. Again it was Lameroux.

"Who called?" he asked.

I explained.

He hung up.

I looked around the station with a sense of betrayal. At first I'd thought it was Betsy's supervisor who'd told on me. Now I realized I was followed from Chastain's office and was being watched at this moment.

I wondered what was in the envelope lying on the

counter under my elbow. I ordered another cup of coffee, although my stomach felt like it was the bore of a recently fired cannon.

More than an hour passed. When the phone rang this time, it was the jackpot.

"Well, hello, String Bean," a twangy midwestern voice said. "I finally got you alone. Your watchdog's gone to pee."

My eyes darted around the station, but I saw no one using a phone.

"You got a message for me?" the voice asked.

"Yes, in an envelope."

"Don't open it now!" the voice demanded. "Go to the telephone booth on Twenty-second Street past the channel bridge. Wait there. Now go!"

I slammed the phone down and broke into a run. I glanced back over my shoulder as I neared my car and saw no one.

It was full dark when I reached the phone booth. A warm glow of light and music poured from a nearby tavern. I stood beside the booth waiting. This time the call came within minutes.

"Yeah?" I said into the sticky receiver.

"That you, String Bean?"

I could hear an echo in the background. My caller was still at the station.

"Yes."

"I know," he lied. "I can see you."

I waited.

"Well, String Bean, why don't you open the envelope and tell me what's in it."

I unfolded the single sheet and held it up to the faint light that passed through the bodies of a thousand dead bugs entombed on the the pale hemisphere. There were

36

two typewritten paragraphs. I read aloud: "I have this day furnished Peter Chastain two hundred and ten thousand dollars in cash."

It was signed by the bank president. I read on: "I have provided the *Tribune*'s publisher with two hundred and ninety thousand dollars in cash. Walter Hammersmith, comptroller."

"Good, good," cackled the voice. "Now here's what you do, String Bean."

I was off on another journey, back to the starting point of my mission. This time Union Station was nearly deserted. At Gate C, as directed, I found a huge whitewashed urn built into the stone bumper by the covered walkway. A spidery fern straggled over one side. As inconspicuously as possible, I dug into the dry dirt. I did not know what I was looking for, but after a little rooting around I encountered a small box, which I pulled out, and then buried the letter in the same place. Not bothering to check anymore for a tail, I carried the box gingerly to my car and sped back to the paper.

A policeman hailed me as I entered the *Trib*'s parking lot and stuck his stern face in my window. I found out later it was Delano.

"You Kingston?"

When I nodded, he said, "Okay, park it there."

I, or rather the small box, was then escorted directly to Mr. Chastain's office. The group waiting for me was smaller, but Hammersmith was at a desk writing, I realized, serial numbers from bundles of cash, and Archie Lameroux was pacing, his hands locked behind his back.

It was an FBI agent, Bob Michael, who took the box from me with wooden tongs, set it on the publisher's desk, and removed the lid.

I'd seen Peter Chastain a few times before but never like this. I barely recognized him. He was huddled in his big leather chair and seemed more wounded animal than an outraged publisher.

"Let me see," he uttered in a shaky voice.

When the tissue paper was lifted back, the contents of the box lay exposed. It was a little boy's wallet, the kind with the edges laced. Inside, dexterously removed, were a few coins, family pictures, and one of those sad ID cards little boys fill out for want of anything official.

Chastain tried to say something but his throat was paralyzed. He nodded. Tears filled his eyes.

I thought with shame of my detour past Betsy.

"These are your grandson's?" Michael asked.

"They're David's."

His arthritic hands paused and then clasped each other as he dropped them against his stomach. "Where did you get this?" he asked me, his eyes still on the box.

"Union Station."

"Union Station," he repeated to himself, still clutching at his midsection as though he were holding himself together like a soldier with a gut wound. Even in my youth I knew his mind was taking him to Union Station, as though that somehow brought him closer to his grandson.

"That will be all, Kingston," Lameroux intoned.

An FBI agent went ouside with me and drilled me for two hours about every face I'd seen and every movement I'd made. When he finally let me go I made straight for the newsroom.

At first glance it seemed empty. Tomorrow's paper was on the presses, I knew. But in the sickly yellow light I could see a few rim men still hunched over the news desk at the far end of the room. As always, copies of the bulldog edition were strewn about. I picked one up and went from the front page to the back. There was nothing about a kidnapping. I was bewildered. Surely all I'd seen couldn't be anything else.

I tossed aside the news sections and tore through the sports pages until I came to the classifieds. At the top of Personals I found it.

"Mr. K, your deal is acceptable. Cash."

That was it.

Lameroux's voice came from behind me, unexpectedly, giving me a start.

"There's no news of tonight's events in the *Tribune*. No one else in the newsroom besides myself and you know what's happening."

"We're suppressing it?"

I guess a certain astonishment surrounded my question.

Lameroux darted a withering look at me. "Mr. Chastain has decided that his grandson's abduction shall be kept from the community until it is resolved."

I nodded dumbly, but since I was also puzzled about something else, asked, "Why was I selected to be the messenger?"

For one brief moment the question seemed to amuse him but he quickly returned to a solemn countenance.

"Well! For that," he said deliberately, "of all the people on the newsroom staff you have a certain . . . peculiar . . . attribute."

I flushed with pride as he turned abruptly and returned to his dark corner office piled high with yellowing *Tribune*s.

For a long time after that I'd preened myself about the "peculiar attribute" that had recommended me to the editor-in-chief. It had an effect on my career, giving me confidence out of all proportion to my age and skills.

It wasn't until many years later that I figured out what that special attribute was for which Archie Lameroux had singled me out. I was ungainly. Too tall, too thin, too awkward, too young to be taken for a cop or to intimidate a kidnapper. What I'd accepted as praise all those years ago had been a recognition of oddity. It eased the hurt some to realize it had been done by a very kind, if strict, man who had almost the same build himself.

I'd been at my desk the next night when the call everyone was hungry for came to me.

"That you, String Bean?"

The voice had a peculiarly intimate quality to it. There was a timbre and intensity I've never encountered since. He told me that he'd put a duffel bag for the money in the backseat of a car parked at David's house and proceeded to outline the ransom drop that David's father should make. As soon as he hung up I raced to Chastain's office. After I'd repeated the demands several times and was dismissed, Archie Lameroux took me aside and assigned me to watch the drop—from a distance. The newspaper at some point would print this story, and since I already knew about it he gave me the chance to cover it. It was the assignment I'd yearned for.

At midnight I headed my car for Ballast Anchorage, part of the port in disuse. I parked on a quiet back street. The only sound was a newspaper sheet drifting in the scant wind.

A grimy fire escape stairway hung counterbalanced above my head. I backed off for a running start, then leaped. My hands caught the bottom step. I felt decades of rust crunching under my fingers, and a grating scream came from the pivots as the fire escape lowered like a railroad-crossing gate.

I clambered up the steps to the second-story landing. From here a ladder with steel dowels for steps led to the roof. This last climb I took more cautiously. The old pins driven into the crumbling brick were loose and the twin handhold arcs at the top of the ladder shook as I climbed. The roof sagged underfoot. A squeaking at a far corner told me rats were scurrying to cover. I worked my way along the edge to stand overlooking the empty street. I had beaten everybody.

Across the way, signs were pockmarked with rust. But I knew which was the old Mendez Bakery. Once an important stop for local Latins, it died with the port after trade with Cuba diminished. Staring at it in the dark, even a teenage boy could feel melancholy that this place where horse-drawn carts once lined up for the morning loaves was now a desolate shell.

Far to the right were the brick low-rise buildings of downtown Marlinsport. To the left, at the end of the pavement, sat an abandoned circus train, a relic of Marlinsport's days as a winter home for one of the big shows of the 1920s. Beyond the train was the old port, now oily and overgrown.

Headlights rounded a corner blocks away and crawled toward me. I crouched behind the parapet but kept my eyes on that pair of beams picking through the refuse on the pavement and swerving to avoid stacks of trash. The car rolled to a slow stop in front of the bakery. Both front doors opened at once and Haskins Delano, the cop I'd seen earlier, and a man I figured was David's father emerged. Delano carried the duffel bag. I heard them whispering but couldn't tell what was said. They pushed against the front door, which gave way easily, as the caller had told me it would.

The two men, drawn together it seemed to me by the need for support, entered the building shoulder to shoulder. Through the grime-caked front windows I saw the blurred illumination of a flashlight dimming to nothing as they moved to the back of the building.

Again to the right a second car, dark, caught my eye as it pulled over to the curb some distance behind the first car with its lights on and doors hanging open. Then at the opposite end of the street yet another dark car materialized. The FBI had lots of eyes on the ransom drop, it appeared.

The greasy bakery window was suddenly alit as the powerful torchlight crisscrossed it crazily. The two men burst out the door. David's father bent over to use the car's lights to read a crumpled note while Delano tossed the duffel bag in the backseat and slid behind the wheel. Then David's father looked up and down the street and jumped in as Delano gunned the engine. The car leaped forward, cut a sharp turn at the next intersection, and raced back beneath me and on toward town.

I hurried as fast as fear of falling through the roof would let me. Over the parapet I dropped down the ladder and to the shrieking old staircase, which I rode to the street—and into the hands of two FBI agents.

Their gruffness turned to anger when they realized I was a reporter. My freedom for the rest of the night was at an end.

SIX

Exotic plants and grasses around the *Tribune* Building trembled in the downpour. One could almost feel the parched roots sucking up water. I threaded the Packard through the Jones rental trucks used to boost the *Trib*'s fleet for delivering the big Sunday papers. They were parked helter-skelter along the river. I drove into the executive parking lot, then swung under the covered loading area to park in the dry, forbidden innards of the newspaper plant.

In the newsroom I grabbed a vacant terminal, spread out the clips, and was well into my story before Paula came to read over my shoulder.

"Lemme see your top, will you?" she asked. Sort of asked. I rolled the story back down on the screen. A devilish smile worked on her tight jaws.

"Good lead," she said, and returned to her desk.

A principal advantage of staying on one newspaper for twenty years is that you know everyone's unlisted phone number and when you leave a message for them to call back they call back. In two hours I'd talked to the chief again, the coroner, the man who'd been Delano's first patrol partner, and the detectives who were assigned his murder case, meaning they got to do the paperwork.

When the telephone rang for the eighth or ninth time, I'd stopped working and was staring out the window at the darkening sky. The afternoon shower was turning into a mean thunderstorm. I grabbed the receiver expecting a forgotten cop to nudge my memory. Instead I got a surprise.

"Palmer."

The gravelly voice was unmistakable. I could almost see his wild eyebrows dancing.

"Hello, Walter."

"Can you come talk to me?"

I looked at the newsroom clock.

"Where are you?"

"Here."

"Jesus Christ. This late on a Saturday afternoon? Yeah. I'll be right up."

I walked to the city desk. "It could use polishing, but I think it's all there. I'll be back in a half hour or so."

"Bullshit, Palmer. You stick right here till I've read it." Then she saw my head shaking no and understanding illuminated her face. "You gonna be upstairs?"

"Yeah. Our publisher beckons."

She turned to her VDT. "Well, fuck it. You don't take much editing anyway." Her young face softened as she grinned and looked sidelong at me. "You really don't, you know."

I took the stairs to the third floor three at a time. Through the red mahogany doorway with its polished brass scrolls I passed into the executive suites. The tile floor gave way to whispering carpet and a line of plantaginea that rustled against my arms.

All the offices were closed and dark except for two—that of Archie Lameroux, now semiretired, and the big one at the end for the publisher.

Walter Hammersmith was the only executive to survive the takeover by the chain. One of the conditions of the sale exacted by its former owner, Peter Chastain, was that Walter could keep his publishing job as long as he wanted it. No such deal was cut for Lameroux. He was still on the payroll, but that was about all. The chain never asked him to retire and he never volunteered, but the new owners effectively shoved the old editor aside by promoting him to Walter's assistant. The rest of the department heads were either retired early or chased off. Then the chain began running in replacements for the replacements about every twelve months. We were already on our third managing editor. The idea of that, so the theory goes, is to keep the *Trib* fresh and energetic. Bull. It's to maximize profits and keep everyone running scared. The best I can, I ignore the chain. To me the *Trib* is Marlinsport and I try not to think about the rest.

The publisher was standing at the bar when I came in. Walter was round without being gross, with a red-veined face that stopped decently short of being florid despite his considerable appetite for juniper. His eyebrows, which bristled like thorn bushes, were so far beyond the mobility and expressiveness of normal eyebrows that it was almost as though he were of another species.

"By God, Palmer, don't you age like the rest of us? You big bastards always get the breaks. How about a martini?"

"I'm still working. I guess you heard about Delano."

"Yeah. Your story's ready for the first edition or you wouldn't be up here."

"Well. The writing's a little rough."

"Bah. Once through the typewriter and you're done. How about that martini?"

He made a gesture toward an almost empty pitcher on the bar.

"Got anything I can put rum in?"

The eyebrows contracted like poison caterpillars. "You and your goddamned fruity drinks. If you weren't so frigging big I'd think you were a pansy."

"Rum's been the drink in Florida since the pirates came," I joked.

He wandered to his huge picture windows overlooking the city. "Ground's dry still," he muttered, looking through the rain-flecked glass. "Water sinks a quarter-inch into the sand and it's gone. What we need is a hurricane."

"It would help," I agreed.

"Scare the pants off the newcomers in the newsroom. All those midwestern editors would be running around squawking like chickens."

His orange soda was flat but I fixed a drink anyway and joined him at the window.

He glanced up. "Palmer, I hope you were able to go easy on Peter Chastain." I reviewed my story in my mind. "There's a couple of paragraphs on the kidnapping. Maybe three. There's no reason at the moment to think Delano's murder had anything to do with that."

"You'd be the one to know."

It was not a compliment, just an observation. Walter had risen to power on the business side of the *Tribune*. He didn't know a thing about what made a good story. But he knew how to make money and he was smart enough usually to leave the newsroom alone.

"I don't know much about Delano's death yet. Not many clues. The house was clean, except for blood."

Suddenly he changed the subject. "That Paula's an exotic little thing. You getting any of that?"

"I never mess around in the office, Walter."

"Now you're lying." He laughed.

"Well, then let's just say Paula's on the way up and out of my class."

"Up? Sure. Up and out. She'll get promoted to another paper, probably the one in Minnesota. For a fifty-dollar raise and a new title she'll freeze her ass."

"Paula's okay. She works hard and plays by the rules. What else can she do?"

"She could stop carrying Moses. Wilson would let her have his job if she could come up with a way to get rid of him."

I gazed at the dripping ornamental tree outside his office. "Why didn't you stick to decent Florida palms and oaks around this building? We might as well be in Pago-Pago."

"Don't want to talk about Moses, hunh? You and your disdain for office politics. You could have been managing editor of the *Trib*."

My gaze slid sideways to the fierce, dancing eyebrows. "Which one would I have been?"

"Haw!" His was an explosive laugh, enthusiastic to its rocky heart, and it lit up his eyes.

"All you ever had to do was say you wanted it."

"I like what I'm doing, Walter."

"Yes. I guess you do. I hear there's another of those famous parties tonight at your goddamned communal palace."

"Sure is. You're invited as always."

"Can't do it. The president's banquet at Marlinsport University is tonight."

"Oh, yeah. They're celebrating that new Olympic pool donated by Artie Brent. Looks like he's on the comeback trail."

The eyebrows nudged each other. "It'll be a long trail with no end if I'm any judge of Marlinsport."

"Artie's okay. He'll survive."

Walter glared at my glass. "Finish your goddamned drink and get out of here. I know you hate long visits to us money monsters on the third floor."

He turned back to his bar and I eased out the door.

Down the hall the glow of a hard incandescent bulb under a green shade backlighted Archie Lameroux in his doorway, gesturing to me. He wore a severe brown plaid suit. Even in his mid-seventies, even though his once-great power was now the stuff of memories, Archie Lameroux was a figure one approached circumspectly. Lean and dry as he was, weighing maybe 115 pounds, still I walked lightly around him.

We shook hands and I followed him into his office, a smaller version of Walter's, tall windows and all. He eased into a high-backed leather chair behind his clean, glass-topped desk and motioned for me to sit.

"Palmer, is that liquor I smell on your breath?" His voice rustled like the sound wind makes in rows of corn in late summer.

"I'm afraid so, sir. But my story's finished."

"Hunh. Seems to me you've started early, even for a

48

Saturday. But no explanations are necessary. I know where you got it."

He studied me with his close-set, frowning eyes. There was a slight tremor in his head.

"You're working the Delano story, aren't you?"

"True."

"His murder stirs up unsettled questions in Marlinsport. It brings back to memory bungled coverage of which you of all people should be painfully aware."

I felt the color rising in my face.

"Don't blush, Palmer. I was responsible for sending a green reporter, regardless of how promising he was, on a sensitive assignment. Furthermore, you shouldn't need my assurance that you've matured into one of the finest reporters in Florida."

"Thank you."

"Despite that incident on the roof."

"Yes, sir."

"Of course, I am not the editor now, and am not supposed to meddle in the newsroom."

"If there's anything you want . . ."

Pedantism tinged his voice. "You know I will never— have never—trafficked in rumors or gossip."

I waited. Whatever was working on him was about to be laid before me. He extracted from an inner pocket the small leather notebook that he was never without.

"The *Tribune* should want to know who profits by Delano's death. His widow? Is there anyone else? Maybe his will contains a surprise. And, of course, there're always motives of passion or revenge."

This was basic stuff. Surely I wasn't going to get a lesson in reporting at this stage of my career.

"Right," I said anyway.

"A civil lawsuit was filed against Delano in the fire station massacre. Find out what the disposition was."

This was more like it.

"Who filed it?"

He glanced down at his notebook. "Lieutenant Maxwell's widow."

"I'll check it out."

"Also, Arthur Brent was once commodore of the Yacht Club. That's a high honor in Marlinsport."

"And he lost it all in the arson case Delano investigated."

"Yes, Brent's social position was destroyed. No gift of any size to the university can change that."

"There are lots of crooks running in Marlinsport society."

"Arson, Palmer, is not a gentleman's crime."

"What is?"

He waved the question aside. "Now, our coverage of the Chastain kidnapping was an embarrassment to more than just you. Owen Blair's denials about the missing ransom money were dismissed at the time as a lie and he served out a long sentence. The last report I have is that he's now in Chicago. You could check that and talk to him."

I wondered why and how he'd kept up with Owen Blair. But all I asked was, "Why don't I fly to Chicago tomorrow?"

A wry smile crossed his face. "They took the travel budget with my old title. I can't send you anywhere."

I felt my face coloring again. This time it wasn't for me.

"Is there anything else?" I asked.

"Maybe. But get answers to those questions first."

"And report to you?"

His face clouded, then brightened minimally. "No. Report to your editors. But I shall be glad to hear of your progress."

I inclined my head in understanding, excused myself, and made for the stairway.

SEVEN

When Henry Mizell designed his mansion around a gigantic banquet hall with stained-glass clerestory windows he could not have dreamed what a newspaper reporter would do with it sixty years later. Henry, no doubt, envisioned multitiered chandeliers dangling from the rosewood beams over elegant dining tables. But Henry was not here any longer. I was.

And the hall was now what a *Tribune* features editor proclaimed in print as "the most astonishing room in Marlinsport, maybe in the country." The furnishings were nothing spectacular, just white wicker, pillows, and plants. What caused the excitement was my collection of old neon. Colorful signs great and small crackled on the walls, recreating in the room a feeling—almost the reality—of a crowded city street from the 1930s. It was a wonderful room for a party.

And tonight's looked like it was going to be a good one. About eleven Randy Holliman staggered into the packed room with two stacks of Sunday papers; one the

Trib, and the other the New Seville *Times*. The music never stopped, but partisans gathered around him, squinting in the ever-changing patterns of light, and devoured the papers. On a library table off in a corner I laid the two front pages side by side. I'd just turned to the jump on A.J.'s story when she came over with a *Tribune* in her hand. She'd changed after work into a pair of black satin pants and a silver lamé blouse, sleeveless but high-necked. I was not the only person—male or female—keeping an eye on her.

"This interview with the neighborhood garden store man is terrific," I complimented her. "He was probably the last person to see Delano alive. How'd you find him?"

She fidgeted as though it were nothing, but I could see she was pleased.

"On Delano's back stoop I found a bag of seeds and sprays. The ticket stapled to it had the store's name and yesterday's date. It turned out Delano was by there a few minutes before the store closed at nine."

"And he described to the clerk a man who may have been the killer," I said. "A nice piece of work."

"Well, as you can see, it wasn't much of a description."

I read aloud from her story: " '. . . some wino bum hanging around the neighborhood,' Delano called him. 'A shaggy-faced guy wearing clothes from Goodwill.' "

A.J. shrugged, a driven woman, it seemed to me, never impressed with her success or satisfied with her work.

"He may have nothing at all to do with the killing," she said.

"True, but in any case it's good reporting. You've had yourself a hell of a day."

She grinned up at me. "I'll agree to that. My suitcases are still parked by my bed."

The way she said "my bed" told me she was almost as

pleased about the apartment as hitting the front page.

"I'll help you drag out some furniture tomorrow," I offered as she went back to reading the *Trib*.

"My editors are going to wish I'd gotten a tenth of what you did out of Chief Salgado and Mrs. Delano," A.J. said, glancing around the room. "And I'd say they are both having a good time now regardless of what happened this morning."

"Each in his own way," I agreed. "Marjorie Delano hasn't missed a single dance."

I twisted around to find the chief. He was in his usual chair, his feet propped up on an ottoman, a drink sitting on the floor by his dangling hand. The lighting turned his dark profile alternately orange and green as he slept.

"He didn't waste any time," I laughed.

"That reminds me," A.J. said, "I owe you an apology."

"For what?"

"Before he conked out, I asked the chief a question about the case and he explained your rules to me."

"Oh, yeah. Don't do that."

"It's a good rule, Palmer; gossip's okay, criticism, arguments, even fistfights. But no reporting at your parties, no working. Right?"

"That's it."

"Have you really had fistfights here?"

"A few. Been in one or two myself."

"Now who'd pick a fight with a horse like you?"

"A couple of bigger horses." I laughed.

"I'm amazed you'd risk damaging any of this," she said, neon turning her smooth cheek into a palette of pastels.

"Yeah, well, troublemakers aren't invited back." I assessed the room proudly. "Do you like it?"

Her eyes kindled with delight. "How could anybody

not like it? But I can't decide whether this is eccentric decoration or evidence of an obsession gone out of control."

"Neither can I."

"How in the world did you get all this neon?"

"I kept my eyes open for remodelings or razings. A few I salvaged from fires."

"I'm not sure if the neon makes the room or the room makes the neon."

"They kinda came together," I said. "When I bought the house, this was divided into an apartment with shaky partitions and a sagging false ceiling. I poked around a little and ended up ripping out everything added since nineteen twenty-nine. Finally I stripped away the black paint on the floor and there was parquet—perfect for dancing."

"And the neon?" she asked. "What got you started on it?"

"Which one was first, you mean?" I tamped down an awakening emotion, not suitable to the moment. "The flamingo there by the chief," I said. "It was in the window of the old Tropical Cafeteria downtown. Somebody I cared about a lot called it the perfect image of Florida."

"I recognize that big one—the Casino—from your story."

My eyes went to the green, turning roulette wheel. "I used that sign to tempt Mrs. Delano to the party."

"I know. She told me seeing it was the one time today she felt like crying. That place must have meant a lot to her."

"Yeah."

"How many signs do you have?"

"Thirty-six, so far."

"So far?"

"There are seven more I want."

Her eyes riveted on me. "I've learned a couple of things about you tonight, Palmer."

"What's that?"

"You're a sentimentalist, and you have a special relationship with this town."

"And what are you going to do with that information?"

"Be envious. And wish I could belong here like you. I suppose it means I'll have to work harder till I do."

Holy God, I thought. If she works any harder she'll wear me down to a stub.

"If I'm lucky," I said, "the *Times* will pull you out of here and put you to work on their side of the bay. Meanwhile, I'm going to keep on my toes or you're going to eat my lunch."

Her fidgetiness returned as doubt clouded her face. "Today I was lucky."

I reached out, took her small hand in mine, and squeezed it. "You know, A.J., somehow I figured you'd say something like that. Why don't we both forget work for a while and dance?"

She looked over at the little band—two editors, a reporter, and two guys from the composing room. They were obviously enjoying teasing the dancers as much as they were playing.

"They gonna give us a hard time?" she asked.

"Probably. They always do."

Sure enough, as soon as the guitarist saw us coming he yelled, "Tuck it in, folks, here comes beauty and the beast."

The band segued into some good old-fashioned rock. A.J. was a bit uneasy until she realized I could thrash around without stepping on her. The music at last slipped into something softer, dreamier, and I pulled A.J. close to me, feeling the tension in her spine. But I didn't get to hold her long. Randy soon whisked her away, leaving me with lots of time to tend bar.

When the musicians finally called it a night, A.J. was still dancing. She laughed when her partner, a TV newsman, offered to see her home and told him she was already at home. Giving me a look, he left with the few remaining guests. I walked A.J. as far as the courtyard and waited while she climbed the stairs to her aerie.

"If you're awake by ten or so," I called, "and if you think you might like a mushroom omelet splashed with Tabasco, tap on my door. I'm a pretty good cook."

She looked over her shoulder, an odd expression on her face. "It sounds nice. But I'm already far more deeply involved with my competition than I ever dreamed I'd be. It was a great party, but I better skip breakfast."

The last was said with an emphatic nod of that glossy head. I forced a laugh.

"You're going to need energy to move that furniture tomorrow."

She smiled, tired but not tense; her edginess danced away on my parquet floor. "Good night, Palmer."

"Good night, A.J."

I roamed the grounds as the musicians loaded up and departed. Everything was quiet out back where the cars were kept; tomorrow I'd have to show A.J. her spot in the long, covered parking area. Her little Bug was still on the street.

I closed up and shut off the power in the dining hall. As I stood looking about the room, in the sudden silence (some neon makes an unbelievable buzzing) the signs behind their railings seemed melancholy and lonely, whispers from the past. I know it was just me; signs aren't lonely. But in the mottled light seeping through the stained glass far above, the signs seemed like forlorn puppets. I love them while the party lasts. But after that they haunt me.

Not that that isn't love, too.

EIGHT

It was nearly ten Sunday when I finally crawled out of bed and pulled on a pair of jeans. I wondered about A.J. and breakfast but it seemed abundantly clear she wasn't coming. I put on a pot of Cuban coffee and stalked to the door to pick up the *Trib* and *Times*. Since I was eating alone I skipped the omelet and settled for an English muffin. I added lots of sugar and cream to my coffee and sat down in the kitchen to read. It was much too steamy and bright out to endure the patio. By the time I'd reread A.J.'s story and skimmed mine, the fog in my mind was lifting.

There wasn't much change on the fronts from the early editions we'd raced through at the party. A.J.'s story was pepped up, probably by one of those self-righteous copy editors with zero street time. My story was as I'd written it. I tossed the paper aside and headed for a shower. Normally Sunday was a tough day to investigate a crime. The town was either at prayer or the beach, but I knew that as soon as Mass was over Salgado would be at the station waiting for the lab reports.

I was going to let A.J. know I'd be back to help with the furniture, but her VW Bug was gone. She's probably been working for hours, I thought as I headed for the Jeep.

I drove straight to the *Trib* and checked with the desk to see if there were any breaks in the case. The early man shook his head glumly. Early weekend duty always seems to bring out the sullen side of any editor.

"How about my request to go to Chicago?" I asked.

Without a word he picked up a memo and handed it to me. The short note I'd left Wilson had earned an even shorter reply: "The newsroom budget cannot absorb such a trip. Make a *few* long-distance calls."

I was not surprised. Getting money out of the *Trib* for anything was tough. But I figured I owed it to Archie Lameroux to try, even if it seemed highly unlikely that a nearly twenty-year-old kidnapping could have anything to do with Delano's death.

There was no phone listing for Owen Blair in Chicago, and the newspaper there was no help. I was starting on the stack of clips on Delano, searching for someone who might have hated him, and searching for the source of his hate for me, when Paula's laughter rolled through the newsroom. I looked up to see her and Wilson coming in together. I figured that was strictly a coincidence, but you never can tell. Wearing an expensive green golf shirt and pants, Wilson was probably putting in an appearance before heading to his club. Paula looked like she was here to work. When they saw me, their course for Wilson's office changed straight for me.

"This guy A.J. Egan really showed you his ass on the garden store interview," Wilson greeted me. "How'd you miss that?"

"I was called back here to hold your hand," I said.

"Shit. I don't want those fuckers to have one god-damned fact we don't," Wilson preached. It was a safe sermon but I don't like platitudes, even on a Sunday morning.

I waved his note. "Then why don't you let me go to Chicago?"

"You know why," he snapped. "So where are you going with the story from here?"

"There's not much new," I said.

"Maybe I ought to give this A.J. a call. Putting him on the staff might tighten a few sphincters around here."

Paula was not the intended target in Wilson's shooting match. Still, she felt the sting and told him Randy was checking out Delano's neighborhood, trying to get a fix on the shaggy character in A.J.'s story.

"Well, that's something," Wilson said. I could see from his expression that the baiting game was over for a while. "Are you working today, Palmer?"

"I'm trying," I replied. "As much as you don't want to hear it, the story may be in Chicago. If that's out I ought to see Chastain about his memories of Delano."

"You can't," Wilson said. "He's still at his retreat in North Carolina."

"Planes fly to North Carolina," I replied.

Wilson shook his head. "I've got to give it to you, Palmer, you are a persistent son of a bitch. Call Chastain."

"He won't give an interview on the phone," I said. "Not anymore."

"I know he's damn strange," Wilson said, "but maybe there's a way around. I'll call our paper in North Carolina and get the M.E. to send a reporter out there."

"Today's Sunday," I reminded him.

"So, they've got people working Sundays."

With that, he turned and walked into his office.

"You staying?" I asked Paula.

She nodded. "I need to hear from you in a few hours. Randy may need help."

"I'll be in touch."

She sighed. "Wonder what the *Times* will have. That Egan is good. You know him?"

"Paula, I thought better of you than that," I said, getting up.

"Hunh?"

"A.J. Egan is one of yours."

She looked blank, then a pleased expression danced across her face.

"Aha! Well, I should have known."

"I'm going over to the cop shop," I called as I headed for the door.

It took five minutes to drive to the police station on the north side of the downtown area. Salgado was in his office. There was precious little evidence for the chief to tell me about. The stack of newspapers on Delano's porch went back a few weeks but he cut out only police stories and none was connected to him. The same knife made both of the deep wounds in Delano's abdomen and the shallow inch-deep slashes in his back. Someone had to harbor an enormous amount of hate to methodically carve up the old cop after he was dead. And so far no one in the neighborhood could provide any real help as to who that might be.

I spent a half hour going over the chief's list of suspects, which included the entire arson gang. He told me there were at least a dozen mean enough to pull off a revenge killing, and Arthur Brent's name turned up again. Then Salgado and I butted heads over the firehouse masscre. He didn't want me to mention it at all, claiming that would only open old wounds. I explained that there was no way to write about Delano's career and not mention that he stopped crazy Felix Pruitt carrying a shotgun in his pickup and let him go because he was a fireman talking about a hunting trip. And that Pruitt went straight to the firehouse and shot up the place, killing three men.

Salgado admitted that the police were checking out everybody involved in that one and he confirmed that the Chicago police were going to try to pick up Owen Blair for questioning.

I got worried when the chief told me an old coot had been spotted in Delano's backyard by a rookie who got excited and called for help. The chief went blazing over there and found a man old enough to be his father, who tried to get Salgado to take a bag of tomatoes.

Poor Carl, I thought as I plodded down the hall and out into the humid afternoon.

I stopped at the nearest phone booth and called Arthur Brent's home. His wife told me he'd gone down to his office for a few hours. I thanked her and headed there. A reporter takes sources as they come. You can like them or not, trust them or not. But if your career is to be more than covering meetings or doing features, you better have sources who trust you.

I wheeled to the curb outside the respectably seedy Stoneman Building, a short walk from the heart of Marlinsport. Once this had been an important structure, but not in my time. The entryway was overdone, filigreed with thick glass doors and brass bars no longer kept shiny. Pushing inside, I smelled once again the familiar peppery presence of dust. The tile floor was white and black hexagons with new white grout patches running here and there like Elmer's glue. I took the elevator—a brass cage rattling with the sounds of chains and cables—to the top floor.

As I expected, Artie's outer door was unlocked. So was the inner one. He sat smoking a long, expensive cigar. A half smile played across his heavy features as he saw me looming in his doorway.

"I thought you'd be here about now." Smoke enclouded him like vapor rising from a marsh. His black eyes glittered with amused condescension.

"How's the family?" I asked.

"Which one?" he countered. It was an old joke with us. Artie Brent had married into the Latin Mafia and did a lot of criminal court business for them before he was disbarred. He still kept this office—he owned the building—despite his employment with a law firm in one of our shiny glass towers downtown.

"Marta and the kids, I mean. I know the others are lousy."

"Marta's better. She really is. Won't quit smoking until I do."

"Then quit."

He frowned and found something else to talk about. "Marta says Archie Lameroux doesn't look good. We saw him last night on our way to the university."

"Where was that?"

"On Bay Boulevard. Walking. God, he must be older than Christ."

"Walking's good exercise. Why don't you try it?"

"Damn, Palmer, any spare time I have is going to be spent on my boat, not risking a mugging on the hot streets of Marlinsport. I might end up like Delano."

He puffed out a wreath and studied me through it. "Salgado's got me down as a suspect, doesn't he?"

"Your name came up."

"I'll be damned if I know what you see in him. He's so predictable."

"And honest."

"So what? This town runs on grease and Salgado's like sand in the axle: he grinds and you always know he's there, but the wheel still turns. You think he's serious or spiteful?"

"I think he's cautious."

"Who do you think killed Delano?"

"I got my list from Salgado."

"Hmm. The great journalist has the where, when, and how, but comes to me for the who and the why."

"Can you tell me?"

"The Torch, Owen Blair, a few others could've done it for revenge. That's the motive. The question is not 'who?' but 'which one?' "

"Who's the most likely candidate?"

"Oh, it's easy if you phrase it that way. I am."

"Is that right?"

"Ask yourself who got hurt most by that stumblebum. I was nailed on a trumped-up conspiracy charge because of Delano's inane testimony."

Artie Brent always referred to his trial as "the conspiracy thing." To him, I guess, it had a nicer sound than arson. But the fact was that in the sixties and early seventies, if you owned a failing business and needed quick cash, Artie Brent was your contact.

"So how come you're suspect number one?" I asked. "The guys who went to prison lost more."

He paled and his jaws clenched. "No. I lost a fortune, and a lot more. Anyway, cultured people feel things more deeply than the masses."

"Your ass."

He laughed deeply. "We need to sneak off for a fishing trip sometime. How long's it been I've been asking you?"

"A long, long time."

"We could go after marlin, drink a few margaritas,

discuss the savage murder of old Hask at our leisure."

"What leisure? There are still a few of us working stiffs who don't have time for cruising around on a yacht."

"I got a deal on the boat."

"You get a deal on everything. Who killed Delano?"

His eyes narrowed. "I already told you I'm the most likely."

"Right."

"But I've got an alibi." A black smile played across his face. "I was playing golf with the mayor. None of the other suspects was, that I can tell you."

"Thanks for the insight."

"Look, Palmer, it's one thing to know what's going on in town. It's another to name a murderer. Motives for those on your list are as common as pelicans on a pier."

He studied the tip of his cigar and I got up to go.

I was at the door when he called my name.

"Yeah?" I said, turning.

"Keep that phrase in mind—motives as common as pelicans. It's a good one. Use it in a story. And tell that hypocrite Hammersmith I said hello. Haven't seen the back-biting son of a bitch in weeks. I guess I ought to thank him for that."

There were a few more editors scattered around the newsroom when I got back. Paula looked glad to see me. After I'd settled in and called the funeral home that was to get Delano's body, she came over.

"Randy hasn't come up with much. We'll go with whatever you've got."

"Did Wilson call North Carolina?"

"Yeah, but he got the runaround."

"This isn't going to be much of a story," I mumbled,

looking up at the clock. "But maybe there's one other angle I can try."

"What's that?"

"It's about time for Delano's favorite bar to open. Maybe I can turn up something there. Want to come along?"

"Sure."

The bar turned out to be a dim, narrow slot in one of Marlinsport's ugly strip centers. Inside it was quiet, no music or video games. The bar was butcher block with a few ordinary neon beer signs behind it. A domino match was being played at the far end. Obviously, it was not a place that catered to the young or the successful. However, it was delightfully cold and smelled of cooked onions. Paula and I sat in the middle of the bar and ordered steak subs and beer. The talk on either side of us was about fishing. With a quick question I turned it to Delano's killing. Several of the old gents tried to re-create their conversations with Delano on the night before he died. There wasn't much. It seemed he was gruff as usual, played a few games of dominoes, and left early to go by the garden store.

One man at the end of the bar pulled out a copy of the *Trib* and began to read my story.

Paula let out a low laugh, but I nodded and listened. It didn't sound half bad.

He read the whole thing and then declared, "Now you know all about Delano."

"Yeah," I said, "except who killed him."

We'd about worked our way through our sandwiches when Carl Thornberg came in and thumped me on the back.

"What ya doin' here, Mr. Kingston?" he asked, then

without waiting for an answer searched around for a stool, scraped it across the floor, and fitted it tight by me.

I motioned down the bar. "Thought maybe Delano's drinking buddies might be able to tell me something."

"I was the one who drank with him." Carl sounded insulted. "They don't know nothin'. Hask and me was the only ones who cared about the news."

"We were just killing time until you got here, Carl." The last thing I wanted to do was hurt his feelings. "I've got a question I need to ask you. Did Hask tell you about a seedy guy following him?"

Carl got so excited I thought he was going to topple off the stool. I reached out a hand to steady him.

"You mean that character Hask told me about did him in?"

"Well, it's a possibility. What did he tell you?"

"This drifter was showing up wherever Hask went."

"Did you see him? Did he ever come in here?" Slowly Carl shook his head, disappointment in his eyes. I felt a bit of it myself.

"Did Hask tell you what he looked like?"

"Sure. He was a bum. Needed a shave and a haircut."

"Did this guy say anything to Delano?" Paula asked.

"Nah," Carl grunted. "But Hask wasn't scared of him. He just didn't like his looks. Spooky."

"What do you mean by that?" I asked, pushing myself away from the bar.

He looked up at me. "I don't know. That was Hask talking."

Paula was quiet on the ride back until we were almost at the *Trib* Building.

"Poor old Delano," she said, "he doesn't even make good copy."

"Oh, I think I'll be able to work up something from what we heard."

For tomorrow's paper I'd go with a barroom narrative, working up a portrait of Delano's mood and actions and throw in the information on his funeral and where Salgado was going with his check of persons connected to Delano's few big cases.

No wonder the pile of clips on Delano was small. It went back only twelve years. I remembered then that when the *Tribune* moved into its new building, many of the oldest records made it only as far as the warehouse. But because of Betsy's diligence I had my few stories on the kidnapping, along with all my early stories, clipped and stored in boxes at home. The only problem was that the boxes were buried in my spare bedroom closet under tons of books and records. It would take hours to dig them out.

After a call to the chief I began to write. I read the story once, made a few changes, and called it quits.

At home, A.J.'s car was still gone. I walked the grounds in the dark. All was quiet except for the faint sound of music coming from an upstairs apartment. I glanced at A.J.'s dark window. She'd moved in two days ago and had spent only a few hours here. I wondered why she was working such a long day.

NINE

I got a nasty surprise with breakfast the next morning. It wasn't front page but it was well played in the *Times*— A.J.'s one-on-one interview in North Carolina with Peter Chastain. It was obvious to me that she wasn't able to get much out of the *Trib*'s former owner, but pieced together with a short bio on him and a review of Delano's involvement in his grandson's kidnapping, she had a passable story. Actually it was typical *Times* coverage of Marlinsport: balls-to-the-wall news reporting with a certain glossy, if thin, veneer of sophistication. There was nothing new on the kidnapper, other than that part of the ransom money was never found and a hint that Owen Blair was probably enjoying it somewhere. The *Times* had to get something about him in the paper to catch up with our previous story. Still, the *Times* succeeded in upstaging us and making the *Trib* look inept. Or at least cheap. As far as I was concerned, we deserved to be embarrassed. We should have spent the money to go to North Carolina *and* Chicago.

A.J. did well getting in to see Chastain at all. Once she talked herself into the retreat, I knew Chastain was too much journalist to throw her out and too much *Tribune* loyalist to tell her anything new. So he quickly went over the known story of the kidnapping. The quotes were strung out well and were probably the only part of the story A.J. wrote, calling it in from North Carolina. The elephantine fingerings of the *Times*'s copy desk were at work in parts of the interview, I could tell.

It was important that I get on to work and pinpoint where Owen Blair was. I wanted very much to talk to him. Also, I had a lot of checking to do on the cases Archie Lameroux listed for me. Maybe Salgado was satisfied that vengeance couldn't be a motive in the firehouse massacre, but festering hate can do terrible things even to good people.

Wilson and Paula were shut off in his office when I got to the newsroom. It suited me fine if the managing editor of the *Tribune* stayed away from me this morning. As soon as I could get an outside line I was on the phone to Chicago. For more than an hour I called every government office there that I could think of, including Social Security, welfare, the jail, unemployment, voter registration, even the tax collector and the library, where I talked the reference librarian into crosschecking an address the police got for me from Blair's driver's license. It was a rooming house. I called the owner listed in the city directory. Blair had checked out several weeks ago. Next I tried the electric and water companies. No luck. If Blair was still in Chicago, he was on hard times.

Maybe he's moved in with a woman, I thought as I hung up the phone. I had gained nothing, certainly no picture of him, which I really wanted. There was no telling what Owen Blair looked like now.

Frustrated, I decided to try another tack. Now was a

good time to check the street talk on Delano. Monday morning the only people about would be the ones with straight heads. I cruised town, but the reaction to Delano's death was much as I expected.

I drove by the firehouse where the massacre took place and chatted with the men. The young ones were glad to talk. Only their captain sounded angry over my outlining the massacre in the murder story. There was pain in his voice when he talked about his slain comrades but only a hint of disdain for Delano.

With the hope that Salgado was having better luck, I turned toward the police station. At the front desk I learned that the chief was at the police academy giving a speech, and the detectives assigned to Delano's case were out. I passed a few minutes with the desk sergeant, who gave me a briefing of the night's calls and arrests. Randy would pick them up. Like everyone else at the station, the sergeant wanted to talk about Delano's murder. Even though it wasn't a cop-killing in the line of duty, the passions were there. It was a mean, degrading death and every cop in Marlinsport felt it. I listened to the sergeant's views and then headed back out into the heavy heat of midday.

As I pulled out of the police parking lot, I spotted A.J.'s car passing with the top down. After a couple of blocks she pulled into a McDonald's. I rolled in beside her. She grinned when she saw me. Her black hair was wind-blown and she looked a bit flustered, or tired.

"Hi, Palmer. You having lunch, too?"

"Listen, A.J., if you're going to endure Florida summers you've got to take advantage of real Florida food. Not hamburgers." I motioned to her. "Come on."

She seemed happy enough to ride in my hot, bouncy Jeep for a while.

"You working today?" I asked.

"Sure," she replied. "I was on my way to see Salgado, so I've got to eat in a hurry."

"Well," I said, turning to smile broadly at her, "Salgado won't be back for at least an hour. You have plenty of time for the best riverfront lunch in town."

Soon the Jeep crunched onto an oyster shell parking lot. Squeezed between two towering office buildings, our destination was an anomaly with its unpainted gray planks and tin roof.

The preposterousness of the place was not lost on A.J.

"This better be good," she said as we pushed through the scarred and peeling doors.

Inside, the first thing that caught her eye was the floor. Over the years, rolls of linoleum, laid one on top of the other, had created a montage of color. In the middle of the room naked concrete showed and the various other layers were revealed in smooth circles worn out from it.

A.J. started to sit down at one of the small wooden tables. I reached out and pulled her back up.

"Not yet," I said. "Come with me."

At the rusty old butcher's counter with its spread of cracked ice and fresh seafood we were greeted by a slender, elderly man with a thin mustache.

"Hey, Palmer, you come for oysters?" Ortega said, wiping his hands on a stained apron.

"Where did ya get 'em?" I asked.

"Appalachicola. Where you think?"

"Gimme two and a water. What're you drinking, A.J.?"

"Coke."

"Coke and a water."

He made out two tickets and handed us our plates.

I feared the strong smell of fish and the appearance of

73

age about the place might be affecting A.J.'s appetite.

"Notice how cool it is?" I asked her. "A fish market is one of the world's coolest places."

When I realized her hand was extended palm up toward me I gave her her bill. We paid at the cash register and sat down.

I took the lid off my half pint of oysters and poured Ortega's cocktail sauce over them. A.J. watched, then did the same.

"Let 'em soak," I said. "The other cups are potato salad and slaw. The slaw's good enough for dessert."

The place was filling up. I nodded at several of the arrivals and caught the eye of a tall man with dark-dyed, slick hair. He came over to the booth.

"Good to see you, *Alcalde*."

"Palmer, drop in this afternoon and I'll tell you about that grant we've been waiting for," he said, smiling all the while at A.J.

I introduced them and explained to A.J. that *alcalde* was Spanish for mayor.

"Glad to meet you, Miz Egan," Julio Montiega crooned. "I have long said that if competing politicians could call lunch truces like the press, Marlinsport would be a better place."

A.J. got out little more than "glad to meet you" before the mayor moved on to another table.

"This is the old guard's hangout, I take it?" she asked, stabbing at an oyster.

"One of them. How're the oysters?"

"Mmm," she managed with a mouth full.

"You've got sauce on your lip."

Her tongue snaked out after it. "Did I get it?"

"Yeah. You're quite the sophisticate."

"You bring me to a joint like this and expect sophistication?"

"Joint? If we paid the going rate for what Ortega's land is worth I'd have to put out ten thousand dollars just to park here for an hour."

"How do you explain this place?"

"It's Marlinsport. The restaurant's been here half a century. None of the glass towers is more than three years old. When the tycoons decided to build up the riverfront— this was an industrial area—Ortega hung on. The real estate agents come through his door once a week with higher and higher offers."

"He always going to say no?"

I looked over behind the counter where the old man was resmoothing the ice, adjusting a sea bass's final bed. "No."

The violet eyes checked my face. Her quick gaze darted to the big front window and read, backward, "Ortega Seafood Fresh Daily."

Her hand fell gentle as a feather to the back of mine and lingered for only a moment. "One of the seven signs you're waiting for?"

I nodded.

She looked at me for perhaps six beats of her heart. "You live with ghosts, don't you?" She sounded so serious, and maybe a little sad.

"Hell, A.J.," I chuckled, "this place'll outlast both of us. What'll Ortega do with a million dollars? Can't spend that much on oysters."

I was contradicting myself but I wanted to break the spell.

"Your house. Those signs. That old car. You surround yourself with the past, Palmer. Why?"

"Are you going to leave that last oyster?" I asked, peering into her plate.

"Are you kidding?" She speared it with the brittle white fork.

"That was a good interview you had with Chastain."

"No, it wasn't," she said around the oyster.

"It did the job. We looked bad."

She nodded. "I think that's the main reason the city editor wanted the story. At first I couldn't figure out why I was rushed off to North Carolina to spend fifteen minutes with a man who knew nothing about Delano's murder, and if he did, certainly wasn't going to tell me."

"It was a damn fine stroke."

A.J. looked at me nervously. "I read your story, too. It was much better balanced than mine. More solid information."

I laughed. "Thanks, but you ruined my breakfast with yours."

She looked thoughtful. "This head-to-head newspaper competition is new to me. I don't know yet how to handle it."

"I think you're handling it fine. Just don't take it so seriously that we can't be friends. After all, we do sleep under the same roof."

"I'm well aware of that. I haven't gotten up the nerve yet to tell them at work where I'm living."

"They'll love it. Ivy Leaguers thrive on even innocent gossip."

"You know your Mr. Chastain was a miserable interview. Once I got by the gate and guards I thought the hard part was over. But he was tough."

"Good."

"Sure. And you would have loved his comment about the *Times*."

76

"Nasty, no doubt."

"More contemptuous. I'm not complaining. He saw me."

"He would. Under those wrinkles and paranoia for his personal safety is a shabby-kneed reporter who stumbled onto Marlinsport before this restaurant existed. He built the *Trib* out of a weekly."

"He told me that I worked for a Socialist trumpet."

"He must have liked you. He's called the *Times* a lot worse."

"Hyperbole reigns in the Upper Bay area: At the *Times* everybody says the editorial page of the *Trib* is Fascist."

I attempted a smile. "We rise to that level only on our more tolerant days."

A.J. stood up. "I better get back," she said.

When I let her off at McDonald's, A.J. made straight for a phone. Checking in with her desk, I thought. By the time I found a parking place at City Hall and made my way up to the mayor's office a good fifteen minutes had passed.

Montiega was as affable as ever and quickly gave me the information about a federal grant coming through for the police department's neighborhood crime-alert program. As I was leaving, he apologized for mentioning the grant at lunch, saying he always liked to give the local paper news first. Instantly I knew why A.J. had rushed to a telephone.

"The *Times*'s reporter was very persistent," he told me. "I know, Mayor, believe me," I agreed. So much for lunch truces.

I hurried back to the paper, thinking I'd better make a call to Salgado before he told everything he knew to a certain female reporter. That damned A.J. was becoming a menace.

TEN

I wasn't at my desk long enough to turn on the terminal before Moses was at my side.

"Chastain flew back to Marlinsport this morning," he said. "He's been on the phone to Wilson for the last half hour. He's not happy about that interview in the *Times*."

"I can imagine. When does he want to see me?"

"Three-thirty."

I nodded.

"Wilson wants you to incorporate it into tomorrow's story—no special attention."

"Yeah, I guess A.J. stole the thunder on this one," I responded. "I've also got a police-grant short from the mayor."

"Any break in Delano's killing?"

"Nah. Salgado is busy but can't tie this to anyone."

"And you?"

"I have a few angles I'm working."

"Including the kidnapping?"

"It should be checked."

"Paula said you'd wanted to go to North Carolina yesterday. Sorry."

And with that simple declaration he went back to his desk.

Keeping one eye on the clock, I punched in my notes and left in plenty of time to reach Chastain's estate south of Marlinsport. Since I was expected, getting through the outer gate was easy. But the dogs, big and mean, snarled and snapped as the Jeep ground up the incline through woods of wild fern and scrub oak. The old man's fears drove him out of town and into this concrete and iron-fenced enclosure ten years ago. Even the grounds were too lonely to be appealing and too fortified to be pretty. It was a museum with only one exhibit—a relic still alive.

A husky young man with bowlegs watched as the animals growled and tumbled around me. I braked to a stop on the asphalt drive. At a word from him they'd climb in the Jeep after me. I kept the engine running and the transmission in gear.

"If you don't call off these dogs I'll have to run over them," I said. "And then I'll want to talk to you."

The sly grin of a born coward crossed his face. He was the type to play keeper to a pack of dogs but not to welcome confrontation for himself. He whistled two short notes and the dogs backed away from the Jeep. With a grimace he motioned me through. I gunned the Jeep into a second walled enclosure—the inner perimeter. There were no more barriers, but the house itself was formidable. The windows looked like they came from the fort at St. Augustine—slits that were too narrow to let a man pass through or even a decent amount of light. They were

79

blocked with double-thick sandwiches of glass. Low arches supported a sloping roof projecting over the driveway in front of the door. This gesture toward architectural unity gave the house approximately the same relationship to Spanish design that a Taco Bell has to a Mexican cathedral.

Two good examples of what slavish devotion to weight lifting can do lounged on the steps. As I got out of the Jeep, they exchanged glances, then moved together to bar my way to the door.

"Hold on there, Freight Train," one of them snarled.

"My name is Palmer Kingston. I have an appointment with Mr. Chastain."

"Let's see your ID."

As I got out my wallet I thought of A.J. talking her way in to see Chastain in North Carolina. That was no small feat.

"The Godfather is expecting me," I said.

The one checking out both my driver's license and *Trib* ID snapped my wallet shut and handed it back to me.

I pushed the doorbell. After a little delay the solid door swung noiselessly open and I was greeted by yet another functionary. Counting the guards at the outer gate this was the sixth person I'd encountered.

"This way, Mr. Kingston," the newest sentinel murmured. He had an aestheticism that suggested, along with his pale skin and refined features, that his work for the old publisher was more cerebral in nature. Inside the rooms were wide. The ceilings were so low, however, that I had the feeling of being in a vault. I knew without looking at a thermometer that the temperature was in the sixties.

"Mr. Chastain is eager to see you," my guide said, and opened double doors to a library. This room was utterly unlike the rest of the house, its walls stretching up thirty feet or more. The high windows let filtered sunlight stream down. The room was warm, which explained the coldness in the rest of the house; an architectural blunder.

In a cushioned chair with deep-cut spiral woodwork sat the earthly remains of Peter Chastain. Before him on a low library table was his afternoon reading material, the current issue of *Editor & Publisher*. He laid the magazine aside and greeted me with a glimmering of a smile.

"Palmer Kingston! Delighted to see you. Sit down, please."

"It's been years, Mr. Chastain."

His enthusiasm was a surprise. Except for the legendary mass firings and manipulations of the news in the old days, he'd almost never had dealings with us underlings on his payroll.

"I long for company," he said.

Age had bent and shrunk him. His face was the color of salted pork. I figured he was deep in his eighties.

"Don't your friends get out here to see you?"

"Bah! The politicians and businessmen don't have time for me now that I'm not the publisher. Their friendships, like the shoreline, change with each new tide of commerce."

"Hammersmith then. Or Archie Lameroux?"

He waved them aside as though he were brushing the air clear in front of his face.

"Walter comes to see me once a month. I am his benefactor, and a large shareholder in the chain, you know."

"Yes, sir."

"As for Archie, I always enjoy his visits but he won't come unless I invite him."

"He's one for protocol."

"Yes, I know. I called him as soon as I got back this morning but he wasn't at the office yet. His keeping banker's hours is a bit of a surprise."

Bitterness exuded from him. I'd better get him on the subject.

"I wanted to ask you, sir, about Delano."

"Well, the *Tribune*'s a day late, but I guess that's to be expected. I never should have sold it."

I tried again. "Your grandson's kidnapping was the biggest case Delano was ever involved in."

"Sure, it was his big opportunity."

I stared at the old man. "I'm not sure I understand."

"Then listen. Delano was a two-bit cop who saw a chance to advance himself. If he was in on solving the biggest crime ever to be committed in Florida, he knew he'd end up being something besides a pavement pounder."

"Mr. Chastain, as I remember it, Delano was only a bit player in the drama, as I was."

"You remember right. But that's not the way he wanted it. Of that I'm sure."

"Why?"

"Well, after the money was assembled and tumbled into that ragged old duffel bag like the kidnapper ordered, we posted a guard on it. Delano 'happened' to be the nearest man in uniform."

"Mr. Chastain, that can't be right. Patrolmen don't station themselves. They go where they're told."

He paused, his watery eyes glittering, and sat that way long enough to make me feel uneasy.

A shaky finger of admonition rose between us. "I am not a man to be contradicted."

"I'm sorry."

"Yes, well, Delano positioned himself so that he would be the logical choice to escort the money for the drop. We were gathered in my office around the telephone waiting when you came in . . . I can see you now, thin as a rail, practically dancing with excitement, telling us the kidnapper had called you."

He stared at me. "By God, you've filled out astonishingly. I guess you owe that to what's her name in classified. Bessie."

"Betsy," I corrected him.

"Yes, Betsy. She's fed you well."

His eyes looked off in the distance, casting about for the thread of his conversation. A.J. was right. He was turning into a bad interview.

"I came in with the message from Owen Blair."

"Yes. I was coming to that. And Delano had stationed himself outside, a vulture."

This time I kept quiet and let him ramble.

"If Delano'd been a better cop, Owen Blair might never have gotten away with the ransom at all. He'd have nabbed him at the park." A dry cluck escaped from deep in his throat.

"Why did you even want a cop along on the drop?" I asked. "Blair might have been scared off."

He looked at me as if I were an idiot. "To protect my money. Why else?"

When I didn't reply, he went on. "As it turned out, Blair raced them all over the county. When he finally did make his move, my son-in-law and Delano just walked away from the money and the damn FBI never saw what happened and that dumb cop couldn't tell them anything."

"Could David's father?"

"Bah! He's no policeman. Besides, he was scared for his son. Why, his hands were shaking before he left the *Trib*. By the time they got to War Memorial Park he was a wet rag."

"And Owen Blair got away with the ransom without being followed."

"He had them walk from the phone booth across the street into the park, then across the ellipse to the shrubbery on the far side . . ."

His old eyes got a spark in them. He was a man who'd spent money grudgingly all his life and insisted on value for every penny. Now he was remembering the night he gave up five hundred thousand dollars to get his grandson back. Two decades later it still affected him. I wondered how often he replayed that night in his mind.

"Blair must have been in the bushes. Probably took the duffel bag the moment they dropped it and turned away. By the time they walked slowly back across the ellipse—at his specific order—he was making his getaway, silent as a snake. It was a good ten minutes before they could tell the FBI what had happened."

"He got away on a bike, didn't he?"

"Rode two or three blocks to his car. Yes."

The old publisher looked right through me. But it passed. He'd come to the happy ending.

"David was dropped off at Our Lady of Perpetual Help in Alverez District. God knows how long he sat in that pew waiting for someone to come along."

"Father Sanchez found him."

"Monsignor Sanchez now." His eyes were damp.

"It was a story that turned out right. Blair didn't harm him and you got most of the money back," I said softly.

"Yes, but the idea that he is free now and squandering my money is almost more than I can stand," he said between clenched teeth.

"Blair always denied spending much of the money, or hiding it, didn't he?" This was the question I knew Lameroux wanted addressed.

Chastain glared at me one more time as if I really were the idiot he feared I was.

"What would you have said?"

I shrugged. "The same, I guess."

"It was a bad time to lose twenty-five thousand dollars," he grumbled. "I'd just signed a contract in New York for that used press. Our expansion of the Sunday paper was at stake."

Strange, it had never occurred to me that the kidnapping could have affected the paper.

"Most of the ransom money was found at Blair's apartment, right?" I asked him.

An expression of pride and satisfaction pushed away the gloom on his face.

"It was David's quick eye that brought him down, you know. And his ears. He told the FBI there were boats near, and then—the idea of it!—by his description of the pattern of the sun shining through the window onto the floor the agents calculated the physical orientation of the abandoned shanty."

"I'd forgotten that."

"It was a marvel. Took their drawing to the Port Authority and using their maps found the abandoned weather station on a small island in the bay."

"And Blair's fingerprints were found there."

"Along with David's. Right. That led the FBI straight

to the longshoreman's union hall and Owen Blair's apartment. With my money stashed in his room. Or at least most of it."

He glared at me. "I have never been convinced Blair didn't have a partner. A lookout he paid off."

I laughed. "Surely you don't think Delano . . . " I didn't bother to finish my sentence because I could see he did. "There never has been any evidence linking Blair to a partner," I said.

"Don't dismiss my thoughts lightly," he warned me. "Even Archie was never satisfied that everything came out about Blair."

I sat up. "He told you that?"

"He didn't have to. I could tell. He was always pushing me to let him put an investigative team on the kidnapping. But I refused."

"Why?"

"I never wanted any of it in the paper, but Archie insisted the *Trib* had to go with the story once the boy was safe."

At the risk of his ridicule again, I asked him why he'd fought printing one of the biggest news stories in Marlinsport's history. "If Lameroux was right . . ."

"Give the kooks of the world an idea and they'll run with it." He leaned toward me and whispered, "David doesn't know but I've always got a guard on him, two when he's playing on the PGA tour. He thinks they're just gofers."

I could hardly believe him.

"That's not for print," he said, straightening back in his chair and picking up his *E&P.*

"Of course," I replied, and knew the interview was over.

As I drove home in the fading afternoon light, I wondered if I had fared any better than A.J. There was very little of what he told me that I could quote. And most everything else was a repeat of what A.J. had gotten. As I fought the vicious after-work traffic, I could think of only one thing. I needed to find Owen Blair— before A.J. did.

ELEVEN

After putting my research and interview with Chastain in story form, I chugged off homeward, dreading the prospect of my freezer's stacked boxes of microwave dinners. Seeing A.J.'s car parked on the street reminded me that I needed to tell her about the covered parking out back. I took the stairs at a good clip, the old wood squeaking loudly under my big feet.

A.J., tugging a wicker couch down the hall, stopped as if I'd caught her at something.

"Can I help?"

"Grab an end."

We worked the couch down the hall and angled it sideways through her door. She'd already dragged in a chair and table.

She wiped her arm across her forehead. "It's hot in the attic. But it's a treasure chest."

"Ready for another go at it?"

She nodded and off we went. After several trips we still hadn't brought all the furniture and lamps A.J. had her eye on. I was hungry, but she was having a great time. While she was trying to make up her mind which dinette set she wanted, I wandered over to the small attic window and peeked out. It was getting dark. I glanced down toward the street and realized I still hadn't told A.J. about her parking space. Before I could, I saw a flash of light and a form closing the door on the driver's side.

"A.J., someone's fooling around your car," I said.

She looked at me for a brief moment, then we both started for the attic door, me in the lead. I practically dropped down the stairs and burst out the door. I crossed the lawn at a full run but whoever I had seen was already pulling away down the block in a dark old sedan.

"What's going on?" A.J. asked breathlessly.

"I don't know."

I tried both doors. They were locked. I didn't tell her I thought I'd seen one open.

"Get your key. And bring a flashlight if you have one."

She raced back to the house.

I ran my hands lightly over the fabric top. Above the passenger side I felt a small cut, just big enough to slip in a tool to flip the lock.

A.J., panting, returned and started to unlock the driver's door.

"Wait." I reached out and restrained her. "Go sit on the fountain."

She started to protest but then handed me her keys and the flashlight. Slowly she backed away, but just far enough to keep me quiet.

I peered in the windows at the scrupulously clean upholstery, then dropped down to look underneath the car. It was built too close to the ground for me to get under, but I poked around carefully.

"There's nothing in it worth stealing," A.J. called behind me.

I got to my feet. "It's a nice little car. Worth stealing on its own."

"It's an old clunker," she said but without conviction.

I opened the door very slowly. There were no snags and no wires attached to it. On the passenger side I went through the same procedure.

"Find anything?" an antsy A.J. called.

"Nope, but let me check the engine."

I pulled the lever and went around to the rear. The flashlight's circle of light revealed nothing amiss. Maybe I was overreacting. The guy could have been looking for stuff to steal. But why go to so much trouble to hide a theft? The tiny slit in the roof and the relocked doors worried me. Feeling A.J.'s eyes on me, I closed the engine cover and walked back around to the driver's side. There sure wasn't much room to maneuver in that interior, but by squatting beside the door and leaning into the floor of the car I could run the light up under the dashboard. In a flash I saw it. A gray cylinder was wired into the headlight switch. It was like nothing I'd ever seen on any vehicle of any era.

"Go in my apartment and call the police," I said over my shoulder. "Tell them to get the bomb squad over here."

"There's no bomb in my car." She was asking for it to be so.

"I don't know what it is, but I'm damn sure it's not part of your car."

I carefully eased out of the cramped space, then stepped back away from the car. "Call," I said. "I'll stand guard."

"Nobody should get near my car," she said.

"I'll make sure. Go."

The police came in cars and vans and the bomb truck. That brought the house to life, not to mention the rest of the street. The police pushed everyone back, including A.J., who didn't want to get far from her car. Quickly an area was roped off. While the officers in padded armor worked on her car, A.J. answered detectives' questions.

TV lights lit up the front of the house like a Hollywood setting and jabbering camera operators shot footage of the bomb squad and then A.J., who stood grim-faced and silent, answering questions only in monosyllables. A young *Trib* reporter tried to get her to tell him who would want to kill her. A.J. just looked at him.

When a reporter and photographer showed up from the *Times*, A.J. finally opened up a bit, but she was as confused about what had happened as anyone else. All she could do was repeat the story of our dash from the attic to her car and my finding the bomb. I felt sorry for her. It was clear the local TV stations were going to play up the novelty of a *Trib* reporter finding a bomb in a *Times* reporter's car. The danger to A.J. was secondary, if it penetrated their minds at all.

The bomb squad detached the device and hauled it away. But the police took a lot longer with A.J.'s car. Before it was over even Salgado showed up in his black Chrysler.

The chief questioned A.J. so thoroughly I thought he was going to get the name of her prom date back in Kansas. There was talk of impounding her car, but they finally relented after lifting every fingerprint on it. I wandered away to move the Packard out of its enclosed garage and into the carport where the tenants kept their cars. Finally I got the okay to move A.J.'s Bug into the garage, which I locked, putting an extra key on her key ring.

Midnight slipped by. But at last everyone who didn't live on the street was gone and those who did were back inside their own four walls. The two of us sat side by side on the steps.

"Incendiary device," she muttered. "That's what they said it was?"

"That's it."

"But not enough to kill me?"

Her voice had a dissociative quality to it, as though she were looking at herself through distant eyes.

"Enough to burn you to the bone," I said, and immediately regretted it. Even though she was in the news business and had to be able to deal with the grimmest of tragedies, I should not have said that. "Jesus, I'm sorry."

I looked down into her sad face.

"What could you say, Palmer? That I might have been burned a little? Don't feel bad over a couple of words, not after you've saved my life, or my legs, or my face, from . . . from whomever. I really don't have any idea who would do this to me."

There was helplessness in her voice and certainly fear, but she wasn't wallowing in either one of them, probably because she was also angry.

The night was warm and dry. The faint rattle of a palm leaf high above was the only sound.

"I'm hungry," I groaned.

She thought about that a moment and then laughed. "Me too."

"Want those omelets?"

"Too much trouble," she said, standing. "But come on up. I'll find something."

She led me toward the stairs. Her spirits, if not soaring, were at least not mired in despair.

Inside her apartment, she ordered me to the couch while she opened a can of vegetable soup and turned on the oven.

"I made cornbread earlier," she said. "Want coffee?"

"If you're having it." The wicker creaked comfortably beneath me as I stretched my legs.

"I'll never sleep. How about milk? Milk and cornbread are good together."

I couldn't remember the last time I'd drunk milk with a meal.

"Sounds great."

The business of the kitchen seemed to comfort her. She put out butter and the milk and sliced an apple onto a plate. Next came the soup, then at last the steaming cornbread in an old-time iron skillet. Since we'd never gotten back from the attic with the kitchen table and chairs, she brought everything on a tray over to the low table before the couch. Then she settled herself deep in the wicker chair opposite, propping her feet up on a stool. She nudged off her white open-toed shoes and they plopped on the floor.

The two of us leaned over the table and started eating enthusiastically.

We talked awhile about her days in Marlinsport. She knew what I was after. But like the detectives and Salgado, I could find no reason in anything that she'd done to cause what had happened to her. As the clock neared 1 A.M. she stretched hard, arching her back.

"I'm as dirty as a goat," she said. "Think I'll take a shower before I go to bed."

"Good." I nodded vigorously. "It's the right thing. Let me sit here a bit longer if I won't be in your way."

She gave me a tender smile that stirred my heart.

The apartment's strange layout meant she had to troop back and forth to get from her clothes in the bedroom to the shower. She made lots of trips for bottles and clothes and God knows what.

Finally she emerged in a cloud of steam, wearing a towel around her hair, a squeaky clean face, cotton drill pajamas and a bright yellow terrycloth robe.

"I thought I'd just sit here a while longer . . ." I said.

"I know."

She leaned forward and softly, right on the jawline below my ear, kissed me. Her right hand rested, light as a canary, on my shoulder.

"Thank you," she breathed against my ear and disappeared into her room. The door closed behind her. I pulled the chair and sofa together and piled cushions under my head for a pillow.

It must have been three o'clock before I finally dozed.

TWELVE

A.J. was an early riser, but a glum one. She hardly spoke ten words to me while she scurried about. Slowly, I unfolded from my cramped position on the couch, my back numb from its torturous night. A scalding cup of coffee got me moving, and mumbling a farewell to A.J., I stumbled down to my own place. I called Salgado. He told me there were no fingerprints on the bomb but checks on the chemical supply houses might turn up something.

"The lab chief's got a hunch, though, Palmer."

"About the bomb?"

"He thinks it's prison napalm."

"That's the crap made with Vaseline and water, isn't it?"

"Right."

"I didn't think that ignited very easily."

"You could ignite water with the detonator cap this guy used."

"The son of a bitch. Do you remember telling me not to be

around when you find the guy who butchered Delano?"

"I meant it."

"Well, you better not be around if I find the one who did this to A.J."

"What if it's the same man?"

"Then I guess we both have at him."

Salgado was quiet on the other end of the line.

"Okay, we've both made our speech to feel better. And neither one of us is going to do anything at all like that and we both know it."

"I'd like to pound the . . ."

"You'd like to but you won't. And I won't."

I stewed over that.

"What about A.J.?"

"We'll keep an eye on her for a few days."

"Okay, Chief, but I sure would be grateful if you'd get to the bottom of this."

"We'll try. You know that."

"Good man. See you at Delano's funeral."

I considered the situation as I showered. The funeral was going to take a big part of the afternoon, so I'd better get something done with the morning.

My first stop was for three apple-filled doughnuts and a giant cup of coffee. Then, in a much better state of mind, I headed for Ballast Anchorage, the marshy, deserted port at the tip of the peninsula, where two decades earlier I'd hid waiting for the ransom exchange. The Jeep bumped to the end of the broken road just short of the abandoned circus train. It was a dismal scene. Weeds sent sturdy stalks higher than the smashed windows of the rusty cars. Paint curled back like streamers at a parade.

I backed away from the track and returned to the former commercial center of this grim landscape, a place I hadn't come to in years. I wandered through the area for a few minutes before I found the old building that was the object of my odyssey, the Mendez Bakery. If I was going to write about the kidnapping I thought it best to refresh my memory. The outside wasn't all that changed—solid yellow brick with small, intact windows. The thick wood door, one hinge broken, scraped along the coquina floor as I pushed inside. Cobwebs covered every inch of ceiling. The bakery no longer smelled of delicious breads, but of dampness and dirt and mildew. I was ankle-deep in litter as I worked my way back to the ovens. The small waist-high doors were coated with dust.

I toed an old Coke bottle, probably a collector's item, but now a roach's home. Thirty-year-old newspapers were scattered around. There was an old placard for Lucky Strike, a Goody Headache Powder wrapper, and lots of Roma and Sea-bo bottles. The place was a time capsule

With a pull on the corroded handle I opened one of the oven doors. It was pitch-black inside. I pulled out the powerful pocket flashlight I'd bought from some cop in one of their unending solicitations and twisted on the light. Its high-powered beam showed a low, circular oven reaching back twenty feet. A small fire pit off to one side was filled with trash. I moved over to a second door, which was half-open, and as I reached for it I froze.

In the thick dust on the edge of the door were the unmistakable fresh impressions of human fingers. Someone else had been in this bakery in the last few days. Even the slowest reporter in the world would recognize that this was no coincidence. This might be evidence. I hurried from the bakery and made for the closest telephone. It took the crime lab only minutes to arrive, with the detectives working Delano's murder just behind.

I told them what I had, explaining that the prints on the right oven door were mine.

They hurried inside.

It was hot in the Jeep. On this stretch of sand and rock there was no shade, only spindly palms and brush. I pulled out my notepad and wrote down my impressions of the old bakery and Ballast Anchorage. The sun was almost straight overhead in a cloudless sky and perspiration beaded on my face. I loosened my tie, but the heat was unbearable and my clothes were soon sticking to the seat. I put the pad away and was getting out to tell the detectives I'd better go on when one appeared at the door of the bakery. He was grinning. "They've got something. Looks like a good set."

I started the Jeep. I was going to have to hurry now. There was no way I could appear at Delano's funeral drenched and smelling like a moldy bakery.

THIRTEEN

It is as certain as a reporter's cynicism that a police officer's funeral will be overdone. So it was with Delano's. Motorcycles and squad cars and the inevitable representatives from other jurisdictions around the state clogged the main artery of Marlinsport for two hours. Delano's religious farewell was given in a big church I doubt he'd ever been inside. But that was the smaller part of it. What took place for cemetery rites was fundamentalist—not old-time Christianity but old-time police doctrine: Delano lived and laid down his life to preserve civilization and no public display of honor could be enough.

When the parade and tributes were finally over, it was time for the rifle salute, the bugle, and the flag. Marjorie Delano, wearing black, but with a slash of electric blue across it, stood stoically in the front line of mourners. I knew from Salgado that she'd refused to accept the flag, and she stared straight ahead while the chief, small and solemn beside her, put out his hands for it himself. Besides police, politicians, reporters, and photographers there was no great turnout of mourners for Delano—a few neighbors and drinking buddies it looked to me, along with the mawkish who show up at all the big funerals. Carl Thornberg was there, and he shook himself loose from his wife and Louella at the close of the service and made his way to cut me off as I headed toward the '56 Thunderbird I'd dug out of the garage for its deep-freeze air conditioner.

"This is not the time or place, Carl," Louella called after him. The bittersweetness of her words seemed to push him toward me faster.

"I want to tell you something," he began.

I slowed and moved away from the stream of police officers on the walk to lead him across the grassy hillside.

"What's up, Carl?" I asked when we were out of earshot. Behind his figure I could see A.J.'s car pull away, one of many inching toward the gate, leaving behind an aura of shimmering heat and exhaust.

"I remembered what you did that made Hask so angry."

"What's that?"

"Something you wrote about bolita a long time ago."

"Bolita?"

He nodded conspiratorially.

"Hask always said he'd get even with the paper for that."

"I never did a story on Delano and bolita."

"Oh yes, you did," he said stubbornly, "and it infuriated Hask."

"Carl!" Louella called. "You don't mean to leave us standing here in the sun, do you?"

"I'll check it out," I said as he turned and dashed away.

I started down the hill after him and met a plainclothes sergeant coming back up.

"Palmer," he called as he approached. "Good send-off, hey?"

"Very appropriate," I mumbled.

"The chief wants you."

"What's going on?" I asked as I fell into step beside him.

"Don't know. He's been on the radio."

Around the Chrysler there was a crowd, which broke apart for me. The grim look on Salgado's face was of forboding.

We knew each other too well to waste words.

"I want you to come with me."

"You got it."

Returning the radio microphone to his driver, he got in the backseat. I took a deep breath and wedged myself in sideways beside him. The car swept majestically from the cemetery and through the town. The driver touched the siren discreetly at intersections. Whatever was on Salgado's mind was absorbing. He was not talking.

"Any word on the fingerprints?" I ventured.

"FBI's checking them now. Could take a day or two." More silence ensued.

"You look mighty grim, Emilio."

"I think we've got some real bad news for you."

"Oh?" Ice water spilled down my spine.

He turned sad eyes on me. "I'm taking you to identify a body."

FOURTEEN

The Port Authority tries to keep the Banana Docks clean and in good repair, but it can't be done. Forklifts back into tin walls; ships sneak bilge and sewage into the channel; sailors, longshoremen, and loafers use the docks and bay waters as a garbage can.

Fished out of this sludge and lying now on his back at dockside, his arms and legs thrusting up into the air like an upsidedown turtle, was the body of the most dignified man I had ever known. A blue and white nylon line was tied around his waist with one frayed end stretched out on the dock. The discolored, swollen face almost disguised his identity but the brown plaid suit was unmistakable.

"Is it him?" the chief asked, his hand on my arm.

"You know it is, Emilio."

"Say it, please. For the record."

I knelt and peered at the bloated face. My throat constricted and I fought for control. "This is the body of Archie Lameroux," I said too loudly. "For God's sake, cover him up."

I heard the air escaping from Salgado's lungs as I rose and walked away. Cops could push photographers around, shift commanders could curse the managing editor, but no one ever gave Archie Lameroux anything but respect. Nobody at the police station. Or at the newsroom. Or in the town, at least not until now.

Salgado murmured a few orders and then walked over after me.

"He's been in the water for days. It's going to be tough for the medical examiner to pinpoint."

We watched as a big yellow walruslike bag was opened and Archie Lameroux's slight body was slipped inside and zipped up. Even in a soaking wet three-piece suit he did not make much of a load. The ambulance pulled slowly away from the dock. There was no reason to hurry.

I turned to Salgado. "Who found him?"

"Longshoremen. Spotted him against the pilings this morning."

"I talked to Lameroux late Saturday afternoon at the *Trib*. He was wearing that suit," I mumbled.

The chief's feet moved nervously. "That means you'll have to go downtown to make a statement."

"Sure."

"It's going to take a while, Palmer."

"You think he was murdered?"

"No question about it."

"I thought the rope, maybe those guys . . ."

"No. The rope was on him when he was found. I'd guess the other end is attached to a heavy object on the bottom of the bay, next to a sharp rock or rusted hull. The buoyancy of his body and the shifting tides finally cut him loose."

I cleared my throat. "Do you know how he was killed?"

"Not yet. But there's so much damage to the back of his skull that a good guess is he was clubbed to death in a frenzy, not unlike the passion expended on Delano."

"There's a difference. Delano got it in the gut, in a fight, however uneven." Anger edged my words. "Lameroux's killer couldn't look him in the face."

Salgado nodded sympathetically. "I'll waive procedure if you need to get down to the paper. We can question you later about your conversation with Lameroux."

"That's all right," I replied. "I'd like to get this over with."

Onlookers could have thought I was being arrested as I was handed inside the backseat cage of the marked cruiser. The male and female officers in the front made small talk while we drove to the station and I tried to ignore the trapped feeling that came over me behind those bars.

As soon as they let me out of the car I found a telephone and called the paper. The newsroom was in turmoil. I gave Moses what I had.

"It ought to be your story," I told him.

"You think I should do it, huh?"

"It's what Mr. Lameroux would want," I said, and hung up.

The detectives quickly drained the few facts of my interview with Lameroux that I was willing to disclose. Then they took a long time trying to get more. But I didn't think I ought to tell them that Lameroux and I discussed my investigation of Delano's death. When they finally gave up and let me out of the small, windowless room, I was not eager to get in the back of another squad car so I called Randy at the paper and asked for a lift back to the cemetery to pick up my T-Bird. Tense himself, Randy filled me in on the shock and disbelief in the newsroom.

"Moses is the only calm one in the place," Randy told me. "He's been at his terminal since you called, pouring out a story, going mainly on memory. I think it'll make the bulldog tonight."

Talked out, I nodded. My own shock was still profound. I needed to get away by myself and sort all this out. But it was not to be for many hours. Once I'd driven back to the paper, I was called into Wilson's office to repeat the grim details of what I'd seen at the Banana Docks. It appeared at this point, Wilson told me, that none of his family or neighbors or housekeeper had seen Lameroux since Saturday.

I went to my own desk, where I lowered my head into my work. Paula came by once, touched my shoulder, and went on.

When a copykid came around with the bulldog edition, I, like everyone else in the newsroom, stopped working to read Moses's story. Wilson stuck his head out the door and shouted across the room, "First-class fucking job, Moses."

The usually intimidated city editor turned to me. "Thanks for your help, Palmer. Your quotes really jump off the page."

"It's your story," I muttered. "And a great one. It does him justice."

Wilson later called a meeting to go over the coverage of Lameroux's death in the final editions. Standing with my back braced against the thin metal doorjamb, I was ready to make a quick exit.

"Hammersmith said it was okay to bump the paper four pages so we can run a profile of Archie's career," Wilson said to the crowd around his desk. "Too bad we didn't get a picture of his body at the dock."

He shot me a look, which only earned him a frosty stare back, and then he turned to Paula for a rundown on page-one changes. For once Moses was included in the proceedings, sitting in the chair closest to Wilson, and he was even asked what he thought of Brown's plans.

"Sounds good," he mumbled to the news editor.

"I had no idea you could write like this," Wilson said. "Christ! You're wasted as city editor."

I'm afraid my groan was audible, although nobody let on.

Paula uncoiled, controlled but excited, from her comfortable sprawl on the couch. She sensed what was in the works.

"I've never seen an emotional story handled with such grace," she said.

I was tempted to tell them to wait at least until Lameroux was in the ground before they started on another grave, but kept still. Truth was on their side. Moses was not good at command even though his writing skills were extraordinary.

"It's not something we'd do right away," Wilson said, "but it's by God something to consider. There's been a shit-load of guys going from editing back to major writing slots."

Thus it was done. I figured Moses would soon be on the streets again and Paula would be city editor of the Marlinsport *Tribune*. No ice and snow for her after all.

"May I get past?" A growl came from behind me. Wilson and Paula scrambled to their feet.

" 'Scuse me, Walter." I stepped aside.

"It's a great tragedy, Mr. Hammersmith, a great fucking tragedy," Wilson said.

The aging publisher looked exhausted. His clothes

were rumpled. His hair was as bristly and untidy as his twin hedges of eyebrows.

"This is a fine tribute to Archie," he said, pointing a folded *Tribune* at Moses, and then at me. His breath was sweet with the smell of juniper. "I want a copy of this paper in his coffin, in his hand, when he's buried."

I saw emotion sweep across the face of Moses Johnson. I understood it. And felt it. The aptness of this tribute to Moses and Archie Lameroux was going to be a permanent thing in the lore of the *Tribune.*

"We are all so sorry," Paula said. "You and Mr. Lameroux were together for so many years."

Walter's eyes lifted to mine. There was resignation and regret in them.

"Palmer can tell you. We had our differences," he intoned sadly. "I think it's way down in the roots of journalism somewhere that the business side and the news side will never really understand each other. But now these petty struggles with each other come back to grind on my soul."

Agitation tugged at the side of his mouth. Even as his face contorted, he turned and brushed past me, across the newsroom and into the dark hallway beyond.

"Poor bastard. The big guys always take it hardest," Wilson said. "He got out of here not a moment too soon."

Paula glared at Wilson, exasperated with him, I thought, but spoke sharply instead to me.

"Palmer, you drop whatever else you're doing and work on Lameroux's murder. The New Seville *Times cannot* get ahead of us on this one."

I glanced at Moses. These were instructions that should come from the city editor. His grimace told me that the publisher's kind words were wearing off and the impact of Wilson's scheme was sinking in.

"Okay, Paula," I said. "What about Delano?"

Wilson, now that there was no longer any reason to stand, dropped into his chair and said, "Jesus Christ, Palmer. We've bumped the dead cop back to the local front."

"No, I was wrong," Paula said before I could reply to him. "Two murders, this close, could be connected. Right, Palmer?"

"That thought has crossed my mind."

Wilson slammed his open hand down on his desk. "What a fucking headline: 'Editor, Cop Murders Linked!' Damn, Palmer, why didn't you mention something to Moses about this?"

"That would be grossly irresponsible. The police don't see a connection at this point."

"Screw them," Wilson said almost gleefully. "We'll run the newspaper. You find the connection."

"If there's one I'll find it. But I'm not going to write it before I do."

I straightened and abandoned my doorway.

"Hey, Palmer, come to the Paddock with the rest of us for a few drinks," Wilson invited as I started out. "I'll buy every drop it takes to fill you up, you big fucker. This has been the biggest news day since I've been in Marlinsport."

"No thanks," I said, raising a hand in farewell. "I've got someplace to go."

Outside the night was hot and the air soggy. I felt its weight on me as I drove home. I put the T-Bird away and checked the garage. A.J.'s Bug was there.

My apartment was hot and still. I turned on the ceiling fans and opened the windows in my bedroom. Tension and heat together were bound up inside me. If I went to bed the memories would come fast, fade slowly. I dropped my

108

clothes in a soggy pile, put on trunks, and grabbed a big towel.

The pool was one of the first in Florida, built in the old-fashioned way with tile and concrete in a rectangular pattern. Columned garden walls draped with vines and flowers enclosed three sides with the house on the fourth. I dipped my hand in the shimmering blackness to check the temperature, then took a low dive off the board, plunging down to touch the drain. I came up, spouting like a whale, and did a few laps past the marble benches cantilevered into the pool's sides and covered with carved art-deco figures the ruined millionaire apparently thought went with the Mediterranean architecture of the house. I agree. The slender naked maidens with their perfectly arched backs and delicate gestures are very special to me. At the head of the pool, beside the diving board, is the largest of these havens. Its gently sloping shape by a quirk of fate seems to have been designed in the 1920s for me more than sixty years later. I sprawled out in it, the water lapping at my chest, my arms thrown wide in a much-practiced attitude, and looked at the stars.

The sky had a deep look; not lights sprinkled across a field but glowing points, three dimensional, hanging in space, illuminating thoughts down blue boulevards to . . . what?

I remembered a desperate night spent not far from this spot—Betsy and I standing between long rows of strawberries, in peril. This was the same sky, but now it was warm and then it had been cold. Deadly cold.

I drifted, as I had done here on a hundred other nights, into a fragile sleep. The water, calming, barely moved on my chest. My hands lay flat on the decking, holding me in place.

How long I dozed I do not know. A muted squeak of

cork followed by a soft pop penetrated my dreams and I was awake to hear a clink of glass on glass and the slow, purring fall of wine.

"Try this," said A.J., her voice soft over the sound of water. A breeze, tangy from the bay, was brushing the surface of the pool.

I took the goblet and turned to smile my thanks to where she sat at one of the café tables. The words caught in my throat when I saw her. It was as though one of the art-deco maidens had sprung to life. A. J. wore a one-piece bathing suit, red and blue stripes on black—a perfectly modest, tight-fitting costume that took my breath away. She was long and slender, and utterly relaxed.

"How's the water?"

"I dunno. I've been asleep."

"I'm sorry about your editor."

She set her goblet down beside me and took a few graceful running steps onto the board and dived in the pool. There was almost no splash, and in the dim light she looked like a minnow swimming off to the far end and then back to pop out of the water beside me on my bench. The water streamed from her ebony hair, straight and squeaky now.

"You could have told me it was cold," she said.

"It's perfect. Thanks for the wine."

She picked up her glass.

"Thanks for the pool."

"A.J., you look terrific."

"That's 'cause the moon's behind the trees."

She had a light way of tossing things aside, but she heard every syllable of what I said and fathomed every nuance. At least I thought she did.

"How do you like my little art-deco ladies?" I asked, indicating the carvings beside her.

"Too skinny," she said, dragging out the "too."

"You're wrong."

"Not enough chest, and they've got boys' hips."

"Don't knock them. I've been in love with them for a long time."

Her hand traced the gentle lines of the figure next to her. I wondered what she really thought.

"Let's swim to the other end," she said, and was gone.

I plunged after her, steamboating it to her darting flashes of color. She beat me easily.

"Some pool. It's gigantic," she laughed.

"Grandfathered in," I said. "The building code won't allow anything this size anymore. You wouldn't believe how much it takes to keep it up."

She rested against the edge of the pool and looked toward the deep end. A row of lights on the top floor of a tall building peeked above the treeline.

"That's the Addison Center, isn't it?"

"It is."

"You ever look at it and feel funny? Or sad?"

I studied the silvery reflection of the glass-walled tower. "Yes."

"It's true, then. That building stands on land you used to own?"

"It was a twelve-acre farm."

"You really owned a farm this close to downtown?"

"We did."

" 'We' is you . . . and Betsy?" She was watching me now.

"Who have you been talking to?"

"A couple of people at the *Times*. Randy from the *Tribune*."

"My wife's name was Betsy."

"She never lived here, did she?"

111

"No. She knew this place, and loved it, shabby as it was in those years. We'd walk past in the evenings sometimes, and she'd look in, wistfully. She never had any idea it would ever be in our reach."

"You had a farm on this island. That's something."

"That side was essentially deserted in those days. Betsy took a classified ad for a distress estate sale there shortly after we married."

"It was her idea to buy the farm?"

I smiled. "Betsy was the brains of the outfit."

"They said you'd say that." She looked back at the tower. "She never saw the Addison then? Or any of the lovely things you've done here?" She swept the garden area with a glance.

"No. She took sick long, long before that."

A.J. touched my arm. "You have a gentle face, Palmer. In some contradictory way it goes with your size. Gentle, but not weak. I don't think anyone would ever make that mistake about you."

"No," I said in mock ferociousness, "and nobody gets away with saying my art-deco ladies' boobs are too small."

Her merry laughter touched my heart.

She popped her head underwater and darted toward the deep end. Halfway she stopped. Chest-deep she turned and waved. I splashed my way out to her side.

Under the half light of the stars and the low-riding moon, with the freshening breeze making her suddenly shiver, she put her hands on my shoulders and tiptoed up to kiss me gently on the mouth, the soft tip of her tongue feathering against my lips. And then she was really gone, quietly, out of the pool, wrapped in a giant towel, to her room. I thought briefly of following her. Not tonight. Not after that conversation.

I saw the light go on in her apartment and knew she was all right. Slowly I pulled myself up and, heart pounding, sat on the underwater bench. For a long time I sat like that. My knees felt too weak to support me.

FIFTEEN

Early Wednesday I climbed the stairs to Walter Hammersmith's office. He was not in good shape. His eyes were a plum color. The lower lids sagged like cups full of thin soup. I'd say he'd spent a sleepless night.

"You're a real treat for the eyes," he grumbled, and punched a button on his phone.

"Gracie, that coffee ready yet? Bring Palmer some too . . . Hell, I don't know. If it's the same way he drinks his liquor I guess you should add a pint of cream and a pound of sugar."

"Ask her if she's got any Danish."

He glanced at me as he lifted his hand from the phone.

"It's too goddamned early for your sarcasm. What can I do for you?"

"You know what I want."

"Yeah, I guess I do. The cops were here last night. You want the same stuff they wanted."

His secretary came in with a tray.

114

"No Danish here," I said as she left the room.

"Be glad I don't dock your pay for the coffee. Get on with your questions. I've got a bad day ahead of me."

"Okay. I'll start with Archie Lameroux's questions on Delano's killing."

"What are you saying?"

"He wanted to be sure Delano's death was investigated properly."

Walter bristled. "Archie was out of the chain of command for the newsroom, and you know it. Were you playing stooge for him against Wilson? By God, that would be wrong, even for Archie Lameroux." His eyes glittered in their red-lined pouches.

"You're not yourself, Walter, or you wouldn't say that. Do you seriously believe Lameroux would stoop to that? He merely gave me some hints to follow."

"What hints?"

"That's what I was getting to."

"Well, get to it. What all did Archie tell you?"

I thought about the question. "He suggested the usual lines of inquiry: who profited, who didn't die. He was interested in the firehouse massacre; whether any suits had been filed or settled or what."

"And . . ."

"Chief Salgado is looking into it. A diagram on his wall places every possible one of those people a long way from Delano's Saturday."

"Un-hunh."

"Then there's Arthur Brent."

"A rat if there ever was one."

"Disbarred but not exactly poverty stricken."

"No." Walter glowered. "Being forced out of his commodore post at the Yacht Club was the hardest on him. But

115

he kept his slip for his boat right next to mine."

"He was on his way to the golf course when Delano died."

"Anybody see him?"

"Later. His foursome included the mayor."

"Jesus, Montiega playing with Brent."

"Yeah. He said if Brent had committed murder that morning it didn't affect his game. It wasn't a request, but the mayor also mentioned he'd hate to see in the paper that he was with Brent since there's nothing to tie him to Delano's death."

"It's the God's honest truth that the biggest and the sleaziest men in town play golf regularly with that old Latin buzzard."

"The last thing Lameroux mentioned was the kidnapping. He thought I ought to talk to Owen Blair."

"Did you?"

"You'd have read about it if I had."

"Can't find him?"

"Not yet. A trip to Chicago would help."

Walter looked at me shrewdly, got up, and walked to his window.

"Today Delano's murder is old news. Let the cops find his killer. We've got a more important death on our hands."

I was silent. Finally he turned back to me.

"You want anything else from me? I've got lots of appointments."

"I'd like to reconstruct Lameroux's movements on Saturday after I left him. Maybe you saw him."

He smiled a tired smile. "Now *that's* an excellent idea," he said. "Ask away."

"Well, I'm not exactly approaching you as an uninformed bystander. I thought you'd walk me through."

"Walk you through . . ." he mulled. "Let's see."

"What about before I came up. Did you have a conversation with each other anytime Saturday?"

Walter looked at me for a moment, his brows drawn. "I think we did. Probably nothing more than a pleasantry since I can't recall any substance to it, but I do remember him briefly standing in my doorway."

"You don't think you talked to him about Delano's death?"

His eyes grew sad. "Since Archie Lameroux was no longer part of the news operation, Palmer, it would have been very painful to him to discuss such matters with me. It would have reminded him of the past, of too much that had been . . ." His voice trailed off and I filled in the gap.

". . . taken away."

Walter sighed. "Newspaper careers aren't all front-page stories and free pussy from the mayor's secretary. There's scut work to be done, and strings to pull and pressure to exert. Archie was a fine editor for the forties and the fifties, but he was trailing in the sixties when you met him, and should have been—if he'd ever given himself the chance—grateful for the change that let him draw a considerable salary for nothing more than keeping his name in association with the *Tribune*."

As if he were reading my mind, he muttered, "Oh, I was in there in the end, one of the Lilliputians binding Gulliver with thread. It was my duty, but, by God, no one can say I relished my role."

I let his words lie heavy in the room before I asked, "He said nothing about the Delano case? Or the kidnapping?"

"If he said anything at all it was probably about the rain. That would have been it."

"Monday, when Mr. Lameroux didn't come to work, did you try to call him?"

"No, I never called Archie. Not anymore." He looked at me guiltily.

There was no need to ask him why.

"One final question. Was he still here when you left Saturday?"

"That's what the police asked first thing. I don't know. His last day at the *Tribune* and I didn't even notice."

I muttered my thanks and left. On the other side of his heavy door there were two businessmen in expensive suits chatting with his secretary. Behind me I heard Walter greet them with an apology for keeping them waiting.

I stopped by the receptionist's desk at the entrance to the executive suite of offices. Archie Lameroux didn't have his own secretary, not since his promotion by the chain. The young woman who answered the phones for him and for the business manager was teary-eyed behind her large, tinted glasses.

After we exchanged regrets about Lameroux I asked her about Monday. "You were expecting him in, weren't you?"

"Yes. I called his house Monday when he didn't show by lunch. Several times. Finally I got his housekeeper. She thought he was out of town."

"So you canceled his appointments?"

She looked at me strangely. "Mr. Lameroux seldom had appointments," she whispered as if she knew a dark secret. "Oh, he would go out to lunch with someone occasionally, and now and then I'd type a speech for him. He still got calls for that."

"Did you keep a record of his calls?"

"No, I have copies of messages I left on his desk when he wasn't in."

118

"May I see them, please?"

"Sure." She handed me a pink-and-yellow-paged record book by her telephone. I flipped back for several weeks. There were very few calls, a couple from his sister, and some from old Marlinsport leaders, long retired.

"He was here most of the time," the receptionist said. I thumbed back to the top.

"You don't work Saturdays?"

"No."

I checked the calls on Monday and Tuesday. There were three: his sister's, Chastain's, and mine. I handed the book back to her.

"Thanks. You didn't put any calls through to him last week that you can remember being in any way out of the ordinary?"

"What do you mean?"

"Strange names, an angry or upset voice. Someone who hadn't called in a long time." I was reaching and I knew it, but sometimes it pays.

She thought for a moment. The phone rang. She took the call, put it through to the business manager, and slowly put the receiver down, her eyes on my face.

"I'm sorry," she said, "I wish I could help you. It's so awful what happened to him. But the truth is last week was a quiet one for Mr. Lameroux. He often stayed after I left, though. Something could have happened then."

The phone rang again. She looked up at me apologetically. I spoke in a hurry as she reached for the phone. "If you think of anything else, call the newsroom and ask for Palmer. Okay?"

She nodded as I headed for the stairs.

The mood in the near-empty newsroom was glum. I saw Wilson through the half glass of his office, a talking head wagging at two listening heads from the graphics department. I had to give it to him. He put in the time. Moses was the only one at the city desk and he seemed eager to talk to me. There was a big wooden box on the floor beside him.

"Look for yourself," he answered my puzzled look.

I peeked inside. It was packed with an assortment of metal objects and papers.

"How about this?" Moses reached down and pulled out a huge old-fashioned photocomp engraved headline. He held it upside down so I could read it: U.S. INVADES CUBA.

"Jesus! Where did you get that?"

"It's from hot type days, made up special."

Next out of the box was a yellowed *Tribune* in its old wide format. Emblazoned across the page were the words JAPANESE SURRENDER.

"You're in there, too, Palmer."

He shuffled through the box and produced a wire service bulletin, datelined New York, that I knew had my name mentioned way down in the body of the story.

"The night you won the Pulitzer," Moses said, "I took that into his office myself. He kept it all these years."

My sad eyes met Moses's. "Where did you get this?"

"Lameroux's sister. She wants me to go through all of his papers, mementos, and files. This is the first box. There'll be more." He paused. "She wants me to write his biography."

"Damn, Moses, that's great."

He shook his head. "It's going to be hard, reliving all those years. I'd tucked away the old *Trib* in the recesses of my mind and told myself to let the past go, but here it is calling me back."

"It'll be good for you, for all of us. It's an era of newspapering and an editor who should not be forgotten."

120

"I may need your help," he said, tucking everything back in the box. "She also asked me to clean out his desk upstairs."

I promised Moses my support and went back to my desk. Only many years of the discipline of writing made it possible for me to work. I sat there, staring at the telephone, trying to decide in what direction to go first. Somehow, I felt sure, what happened to Delano was connected to Lameroux's death. I dialed the police station.

Salgado was not in a very good mood. Two unsolved murders and a car bombing were grating on him.

"Can't find anyone who saw him at the docks," he grumbled.

"He walked almost every night on Bay Boulevard," I told him. "Could he have been robbed?"

"No robber ever left behind a watch, a gold ring, or a wallet with over a hundred bucks in it."

"No notebook?"

"No."

"Has the time of death been fixed?"

"The best the medical examiner can do is a sloppy guess at late Saturday—early Sunday."

"Leaves a lot of room."

"Yeah."

"What about his family? Why wasn't he missed?"

"His sister was at her beach cottage over the weekend."

"Neighbors?"

"You know what it's like in a condominium. Nobody knows what anybody else is doing. You got anything?"

"I'm just getting started."

"Swell, we're both spinning our wheels. Maybe I ought to just go on what that A.J. had in the *Times* this morning."

I had a sinking feeling in the pit of my stomach. "What do you mean?"

"You haven't read the *Times*?"

"No."

"She asked me about the Delano murder yesterday. Wanted to know if there was a connection."

"And?"

"I told her it was possible. She ran with it."

"I see."

"But there is not a shred of evidence linking Delano in any way with Lameroux. If I'd known what she had in mind, I'd have been a bit more careful. When we find these killers, and we will, I guess she'll say then how wrong I was to think they were connected. Damn reporters."

I was beginning to understand the chief's bad mood a little better. Mine also was taking a plunge.

"Any word of the fingerprints?"

"Not yet."

"You will call me first on them?"

"On my word," he said, and hung up.

SIXTEEN

The *Tribune*'s conference room always has copies of the *Times* laid out next to the *Tribune* on a long table. Editors agonize over them daily. I picked up the final of the *Times*. A.J.'s lead made the connection of the two murders happening on the same day; her second paragraph quoted Salgado's "possible" same killer; and her third said there were few clues to the suspect. She gave a veiled description of Lameroux's body on the Banana Docks, a few paragraphs of praise for his contributions to journalism, and a rehash of the Delano killing and her interview with Chastain. She closed with a quote from Salgado in response to her question did he think the killer would strike again.

"How can I answer that?" he said.

The *Times* ran a ten-year-old picture of Lameroux out front and the same ancient prison mug shot of Blair on the jump they'd used Monday. I tossed the paper back on the table. No doubt Wilson and Paula would be on me soon. There was no attempt to tie the murders together in the *Tribune* other than a paragraph I'd given Moses saying it was within twenty-four hours of the time Delano was killed. Of course, Moses's story was by far the best piece in either paper, but that's not what Wilson would want to talk about. From all appearances, the *Times* was ahead of us on the story, and my evaluation of the evidence and coverage of the funeral could not make up for that. Facts be damned. I couldn't help but wish the *Times* was more interested in investigative reporting than titillating speculations. But, however she had arrived there, A. J. was writing what I was carefully trying to check out. I felt like a mule in a race with a greyhound.

If I was going to be a plodder I decided at least I'd plod in a straight line. I went to the guard station where Smitty was on duty.

"Can I see the Saturday pages in the registration book?" I asked.

"I figured you'd come."

Wonderful, I thought. Even the security guards are out in front of me.

I skimmed down the row of names. None of them checked in to see Lameroux, none raised suspicions.

"Do you remember what time Mr. Lameroux left Saturday?" I asked.

"I didn't check my watch, but I'd say between six and seven—before dark."

"Can't you do better than that?" I prompted. Seven o'clock would make it a good hour after I talked to him.

"No. All I can remember is first he left, then Mr. Hammersmith came down shortly thereafter with Mr. Wilson and that redhead with the body."

"Paula Prince."

"Yeah." He grinned.

"Did Mr. Lameroux say anything to you?"

"I've been thinking about that, and the way he was," Smitty replied. "He's one for formalities, you know. I mean, he was."

"It catches us all. What'd he say?"

"Well, Saturday, he almost was out the door before he turned back and wished me a good evening . . . Something was on his mind. His face was drawn. I think there was a tremor to his hands. You know he did that when he was tense. Palsy, I think. My father has it."

"He didn't say anything else."

"No, that's what I mean. It was as if he didn't even see me. Glanced my way out of habit, then realized what he was doing as he pushed out the door and turned back."

"And you don't know what time it was?"

"Not to the minute, no."

"Thanks, Smitty."

I drove to the nearest phone booth and called Lameroux's sister. She was the only family he had in town. Like me, he'd lost his wife years ago and his children were scattered. I discovered they were all at their aunt's house. I apologized for bothering her but she told me her brother thought highly of me and she couldn't imagine not cooperating.

But her willingness led nowhere. She knew of nothing her brother was concerned about. No, he hadn't told her of any threats. No, she didn't know if he had any plans Saturday night.

"Normally," she told me as I was about to give up, "if he didn't have an engagement he'd walk down to the Columns for a seafood dinner and then walk back to the newsstand to pick up the early editions. You know he never could get very far from the paper." Her voice broke. "He was an old man, Palmer, who lived in the past."

125

I didn't know what to say.

"You find the person who did this awful thing," she cried.

"I'll try," I mumbled. "I loved him, you know."

"God bless you," she said, and hung up.

Back in the Jeep, I switched on the radio loud and tried to insulate my brain with pounding music as I headed for Bay Drive. At that hour the Columns' parking lot was empty. I parked and walked up the zigzagging ramp to the restaurant, a rambling version of a thirties sea shanty, and rapped hard on the door. No one answered. A delivery truck swung around to the back and I followed. Once in the kitchen I got directions to the manager's office.

Mildred Carter greeted me with a friendly handshake and an offer of coffee and blueberry muffins. I took her up on both and she led me into the empty restaurant and set up a place for us at a vast window overlooking the bay. A middle-aged woman with short, graying hair, Mildred was easy to like and to listen to. She really knew Archie Lameroux.

"My waitressess would compete to serve him." Her voice was thick with emotion. "I tell you, Palmer, this place won't be the same without him. He was as much a part of the Columns as . . . as the bay out there." She sighed and leaned back. "But God, I'm glad I knew him."

"Were you here Saturday night?" I asked her.

"Sure was. I looked for Mr. Lameroux. We had crab legs, his favorite—but he never showed. You don't think that's when . . ."

"Did he have a reservation?"

"No, in the last years he mostly came alone, or with his children when one was in town. But I don't think he was

126

unhappy. He liked to talk about the old days. He had some great stories."

And she proceeded to tell me a couple of them. Being with her was therapeutic for me. In my mind for the first time I got beyond the yellow body bag and got back Archie Lameroux. I thanked her sincerely for her time and the muffins—I'd emptied the platter—and went out into the bright sunlight. A small breeze off the bay tempered the heat. I decided to walk up the boulevard to Lameroux's condominium. I crossed the divided street to the wide sidewalk and low wall that ran miles along the water. It was a favorite path for all kinds of people—joggers, lovers, mothers with baby carriages, old folks with lots of time on their hands to watch other people. That Lameroux could have been attacked or forced into a car without someone seeing it seemed unlikely.

I walked at a fairly slow clip, trying to match my long legs with the time it would take a smaller, older man to make the trip. An unmarked police car cruised by. As I neared the towering building Archie Lameroux had called home, I saw the teams of detectives Salgado had working the neighborhood.

I recrossed the street and checked my watch as I came up to the lobby. Eleven minutes had passed. The doorman/guard had what I wanted.

Archie Lameroux left the building alone and on foot as Arthur Brent had told me at approximately 7:15. The guard was sure of the time because it was a few minutes after he showed up for work late that Lameroux came down—wearing a brown plaid suit. The guard also said that there was a good number of people out that night enjoying the sunset despite the threatening weather.

I called Paula on the walk back to my Jeep.

She wanted a story out of me on Lameroux's murder right away. "I thought you and Salgado were buddies," she said. "How come he's giving everything to A.J.?"

"He didn't give her anything," I said, "she's asking."

"And you?"

"Come on, Paula, you read her story. What did you find out?"

"Okay, I don't want to argue with you. I know you're busting your ass, but this thing is big. We're getting requests for anything we can come up with for the national wire. And the networks are calling us."

"Have I gotten any calls from Chicago?"

"One. From your contact at the *Times*. The word on Blair is that they think he skipped."

"Damn."

"What are you going to do now?"

"Going to get some quotes from Salgado, what else?"

So I went to the police station, where I saw A.J.'s little Bug parked. Although I was not all that eager to talk to her I was glad to know she was all right. A car bombing her first week in town was not exactly a greeting from Welcome Wagon. It suddenly occurred to me as I walked by her car that neither the police nor myself were trying very hard to find the bomber. I'd better talk to the chief about that, I thought as I greeted the desk sergeant.

"He's got somebody with him," I was quickly informed. I grinned. "I know. How long she been there?"

"Ten minutes."

"So, anything happening?"

"No more murders, just a barroom shooting."

His telephone rang. I stretched out on one of the hard

chairs against the far wall. Locking my fingers behind my head, I settled back to wait. The next thing I knew something was kicking me softly. I opened one eye and looked up at A.J.'s cheerful face.

"Palmer," she said, "I'm glad to see you. You hungry? How about lunch at Ortega's?"

She really did sound glad to see me. I stood up. "Can't. I've got to see the chief," I said. "Hey, I thought this was your day off."

"It's supposed to be, but there's too much going on. I couldn't stay home," she said, starting for the door. "See you later."

The chief grumbled when he saw me. "Reporters must think I've got nothing better to do all day than talk to them."

"Salgado, you love it."

And talk he did. He went over every name mentioned in connection with both murders, every scrap of evidence, every alibi. It was obvious the investigations were thorough but stalemated.

"Hell, Palmer, you ready to join the chorus about the police department's inability to catch a mad killer?"

"Is that what A.J. did?"

"Close enough," he grumbled. "I know her bosses put her up to it, but now the TV stations are demanding action, whatever the hell that is. Maybe they think I should go out and beat a confession out of some wino."

"Did the medical examiner find anything to tie Lameroux's death with Delano's?"

Slowly he shook his head.

"Got a good impression of the shape of the injury to his brain, which will be evidence if and when we find the weapon. Some kind of cylinder, almost like a big rolling pin. But the body was in the water too long for any traces of lint or hair or skin under the nails."

When the chief's telephone rang I stood to go.

"Yes, sir," I heard him say, "I've been waiting for your call . . . right . . . you're sure?" His voice was tense. "Yeah, thanks a lot. For questioning . . . Right . . . I'll call. Goodbye."

The receiver dropped with a rattle as Salgado raised his eyes to mine.

"Owen Blair," he said with clenched teeth. "That was the FBI. It was Owen Blair at the bakery."

SEVENTEEN

Dark, rolling clouds stretched that afternoon in a long, mean line, across the bay and south toward the gulf. Cold drops of fresh water mixed with the sting of salt spray in my eyes as the powerboat scooted under Bayway Bridge. Far to starboard an inbound ore carrier steamed high in the water toward the phosphate terminals. Nearer at hand and to port was a coal barge, wallowing deep, headed for the power plant. I cut right to give him room.

The boat was borrowed from the Port Authority. Crime is not unknown on the docks at Marlinsport, so neither am I. Over the years I've come to know most of the principals and even more of the grunts that work the ships coming and going with cargoes of cars, citrus, phosphate, and petroleum, plus an occasional shipment of cocaine.

Thunder cracked around me. I nudged the twin throttles a little and the big boat sliced through the wavetops. My destination was Sanctuary Island, home for one of the oddest, richest, and most exclusive organizations in the Marlin Bay area—the Harbor Pilots.

The men who guide the vessels into Marlinsport pay

the highest initiation fee I've ever heard of, and money alone won't do it. They must also know the bay and its reaches, and the only way to learn is as a pilot's assistant. Thus, the pilots have iron control over who shares in the six-figure incomes and who gets to enjoy lobster lunches on their three-day on/week off shifts.

As I approached the island's overbuilt dock, I spied Jack Betancourt, president of the Harbor Pilots, standing there, slickered but bare-headed. Britain was stealing tea from China when Jack was born, and they say he is still capable of bringing a full-rigged East Indiaman to the wharf under sail. His hair stuck out in wet gray cowlicks as he watched my docking in the storm.

"You're getting rusty," he called.

"You're getting wet," I yelled back, wrestling with the line.

He didn't move, just stood staring down at me as I swarmed over the dock. At last the Port Authority's boat was secured, and I hopped up beside him. The rain was cascading off my chin.

I grinned foolishly. "Hey, Jack," I said, "I'm here to pick your brain."

We walked side by side up a planked path to the bone-colored building with its rooftop captain's walk and cupola.

Inside, after shaking out his slicker and hanging mine beside it, Jack settled his thick body into a good leather chair behind a table with a chart of the bay spread on it.

"Never met Lameroux," he said. "Doubt if I can help you."

I bent over the chart. Penciled notations were scrawled all over it—the locations of recent wrecks, stumps, and worksites.

"His body was found here," I said, pointing to the northeastern area of the port.

"Banana Docks?"

"Pier Two to be exact."

Jack shoved himself up from his comfortable chair without a word and stomped off through a rear door. He was, I knew from previous visits, heading for the kitchen. And I knew what for.

He came back grumbling and tearing the top off a box of Cheez-its. He crammed a handful in his mouth, shook a big pile into my hand, and collapsed back into his chair.

"Where'd he disappear from?"

I shoved the crackers in my mouth and put my left index finger on the shoreline near the Columns.

Jack rubbed his chin.

"How long was the slack end of that line tied around him?"

"Maybe three feet from the knot."

The old seaman's dark-creased finger slid along the western edge of the water, where it touched the eastern edge of the peninsula.

"This is damned near a mudflat. It's all shallows from the bridge south. You'd have to use a backhoe to dredge a spot deep enough to hide a body."

He dipped into his Cheez-its box and munched thoughtfully, staring at the chart.

"He came in on the morning tide, right up Harrison Channel. Sorry to be so graphic. I guess he was your friend."

"Somebody I cared a lot about."

He crunched crackers slowly. "The same thing's true on the east side—shallows. Complicated to a very considerable degree by mangroves."

"What about the Bayway Bridge? Could the body have been dropped from there?"

"You're the newspaperman. You tell me. Where do all the suicides show up?"

"The New Seville side of the bay. Far away from the Banana Docks. Could a body be dropped from any of the other bridges and float to the Banana Docks?"

"I don't want to be indelicate, Palmer, but you'd have to mount an outboard on a body to make it travel any such route as that. You'd fight tides, winds, even the outflow of the river. No. That's not what happened."

"What did happen, Jack?"

After peering in the box, he shook me out a small share of Cheez-its.

"Somewhere here, in the deep blue, is where he was dropped." He swept a rough hand along the shipping lanes. "Three feet of line, or twenty, in here and you'd never see a body again. Anywhere else and it would be like setting out a buoy."

"From a boat then," I said.

"Or a helicopter. And . . . there's one place on the shore he could have been tossed in." He was gazing at the chart, his head cocked. I looked where he was looking.

"Coquina Point?"

"It's isolated, there's deep water right up to the seawall. How big was this editor?"

"Very slight."

"Then he'd be easy to heave off, weight and all."

"You think a ship's screw cut the line?" I asked.

"Not if your editor was in one piece. He was, wasn't he?"

I nodded.

"Then the line around him probably rubbed against coquina out in the channel until it frayed and he popped to the surface."

I peered out the heavily cross-hatched window.

"Don't look so disappointed, Palmer. I've eliminated every place but two."

"Yeah, thanks . . . Weather's eased."

"Good." He shook the empty cracker box.

"I'll be shoving off."

As I dashed down the boardwalk, the wind and fragments of raindrops swept against me. I could see Jack watching from the window.

The boat's engines throbbed to life and I cast off, easing gently astern, then slid away. Even throttled back for the run with following seas, the boat moved quickly. I shot under the big bridge, then cut to starboard to the shallows off the East Bay bulge. As the boat coursed northward I wondered why Owen Blair was in town and wished I knew what he looked like now. Finding him was not going to be easy without a more recent photograph. Right now he was the closest thing to a suspect. One thing for sure was that an ex-longshoreman like Blair would know where to dump a body. But why would Archie Lameroux get in a car with the old kidnapper?

When I returned the boat, I checked the Authority's logs. The *Eccles Champion* of Monrovian registry was moored from Saturday early through Monday at Coquina Point unloading a cargo of gasoline. That cargo would call for a watch around the clock. A man lugging a body would play hell getting past. Thus, one of Jack Betancourt's two possibilities was out.

Archie Lameroux's body was thrown in the bay from a boat.

It was time to get back to the paper to write the story on Lameroux's last day alive, and also to tell the citizens of Marlinsport that Owen Blair was back in town.

EIGHTEEN

Despite the noisy comings and goings of tenants, the house seemed lonelier than usual. I heated macaroni and cheese and reopened a container of soupy three-bean salad bought a couple of weeks before A.J. moved in. Neither the macaroni nor the salad was good and the iced tea had a film on top of it. I drank it anyway, to wash down the other.

The long summer twilight lured me back outdoors. I cranked up the Packard after noting that A.J.'s VW was still missing from the garage and tooled around to the front and parked on the brick circle by the fountain. Only minor tinkering was needed but it had to be done by tomorrow, for Lameroux's funeral. I'd decided that the Packard was the only suitable car for me to drive because Lameroux had really liked it. He'd told me once he knew—by reputation only—the gangster to whom it originally belonged. The lights in A.J.'s apartment stayed dark.

Across the way, frogs started their nightly chant in a large shallow pond with enough lily pads in it to resurrect Monet. As the light faded, the noisy crickets in the lawn joined them, a wonderful loud lonely song.

At the paper they'd liked my story about Lameroux. Nothing sappy, just a straightforward account of his day up until the time he disappeared from Bay Boulevard, and I laid out my conclusions as to where his body had been dropped in the bay. High up in the story I had revealed that Owen Blair was back and the police wanted to question him.

I put my tools away and cranked up the Packard again, rolling down the short brick drive and through the arched gateway to the street. I drove a few blocks toward town but there was no sign of A.J.'s little Bug. I turned back and pulled in behind the house. Knowing how foolish it was, I peeked in the garage to see if the VW was there. Of course it wasn't.

It grew dark. Back in the house I switched on the TV long enough to cycle through everything from Channel Three to Channel Fifty. Games, guns, and commercials. I thought about hitting the bars by the port but I knew Blair wouldn't be going by his own name and there was no way I'd recognize him. Tomorrow I'd ask a few questions at the longshoreman's hall and the blood banks.

Somehow I found myself in the old banquet room. Moonlight peeked palely through the high windows. Idly, for no good reason, I turned on all the neon signs. Some fizzed and some winked but they all eventually came on. My boating shoes squeaked on the gleaming floor as I crossed to a chair. I sat down and let my eyes wander around the room.

In life, the flamingo gets its color from the pink crustaceans it sifts in the shallows. It is a delicate color laid on by years and diet.

In neon, the artisan uses a special powder to get the

137

color wanted. My flamingo stood in a rippled line of blue neon water, beside a green and yellow sago palm. The flamingo's rosy pink was too garish for life, too vivid. But against the other colors it had to have an extra infusion of red to hold its own.

A little after ten I took a walk around the block. I ducked out the back door, checking the garage for security, then made my loop. Coming back I saw that all the windows up top were still dark.

I slammed into the apartment and punched up the city desk. "Hey, this is Palmer. What the hell's going on in town tonight? What's working?"

"Gee, I dunno. Rick's in the slot. Wanta talk to him?"

A little wait.

"Hi, Palmer. Anything up?"

"I was gonna ask you."

"Ummh. No. Nothing from the cops at all—oh, they're pulling traffic duty over on East Seventh Street. There's a paint warehouse burning out of control. Say, the news desk is tickled with your story on Mr. Lameroux. It's the overplay on one."

"Where on Seventh?"

"At Nevada."

I slammed down the phone and legged it out back to the Jeep.

I shot through town and under the expressway, then bore right toward the black and orange flames pulsing over the Alverez District. As soon as I got to where the hoses were snaking all over the street I bumped up onto the sidewalk and cut the engine.

Paint warehouse it might be now, but the roaring building once was a cigar factory. Scores of them dot the district, some abandoned, but most converted to other uses.

138

The smell of cigars permeates even the funeral business in Marlinsport. All of our best coffins come from two of the old brick buildings. This one would no longer be used for anything. Flames spewed from every window like dragon-breath. Oily, rolling smoke smothered the roof, letting only the hottest licks of flame burst through. The street was a glittering mass of fire engines. The grind of the engines and roar of the water combined with the fire itself to set up a tremendous din. A cluster of still photographers and tele-vision camera operators broke suddenly and ran pushing and yelling past me. Their departure revealed the smaller figure of A.J., notebook in hand, quizzing a captain. I drifted over.

"Hi, Cliff"

"Jesus, Palmer! Haven't seen you at a fire in a long time," he yelled at me. "Do you know something I don't?"

"Not a thing," I muttered. "Hello, A.J."

"Hi, Palmer. The near wall's about to come down, the captain says."

"Yeah, I saw the photographers running for side angles."

She'd been working the fire too close. There was an apple-cheeked burn on her face.

A great snapping came as old wooden beams pulled apart and the wall began to sag.

"Get behind that pumper," the captain ordered at the top of his voice. "This is it."

The drooping lip in the middle of the wall slipped lower. In two great pieces it came down. The bricks hitting the street sounded like falling bamboo. Water immediately spurted into the burning core of the building from firefigh-ers stationed like the photographers at either end.

"There won't be much left," A.J. shouted.

"Well, if we're energetic enough we can still save the vacant lot," the captain said. His eyes slid to A.J.

He grinned. "Don't quote me on that one."

Behind us a crowd was held back by a police line of yellow tape strung between power poles. There were the usual faces, winos from the neighborhood, teenage boys and girls cruising for any action, and probably some businesspeople whose own livelihoods were being menaced by the flames. One big geek with an adam's apple like a coffee spout was ogling A.J. My eyes roamed over the rest of the crowd and focused back on the fire. After a couple of minutes I turned to the crowd again. He was still staring at her with an intensity that bordered on obsession. I tried to read the emotions on his lined, long face. I didn't know if it was anger I saw, or lust, or plain meanness. I started over to talk to him. His eyes darted to mine and he tried to brazen it out. But as I neared him his gaze dropped and he edged back into the crowd. When I reached the yellow line I could see over the heads that he was getting into an old green Chevy. As it pulled away I wondered if the seedy middle-aged derelict could have set the blaze. If there is any evidence of arson, I'm going to blame myself for not following him, I thought. As I walked back toward A.J. I figured chances were he was just one of those creeps who think love and pussy are the same thing, and maybe fire too.

Black ash was settling on A.J.'s white cotton blouse. Flecks of dust and cinders dotted her shiny face. Her black loafers and the bottom eight inches of her slacks were soaking wet. I smiled at her.

By midnight the fire marshal and others were picking over the wreckage of the building, seeking their clues, hoping they wouldn't find any bodies. They didn't. A.J. up dated her story and raised an amused eyebrow when she saw I wasn't going to file one at all.

"There's a café open not far from here. Join me?"

She looked down at herself. "Not tonight. Not like this. They'd want to hose me down at the door."

"Nah. These folks know reporters. They're friends of mine," I pressed her.

"No," she said emphatically. "I'm going home and clean up. Bleah! My shoes feel like they've got fish in them."

"You are a soggy sight," I agreed. I watched her get into her car, which was parked beside a police vehicle. Not much danger there; still I was glad when the engine churned up. She backed into the street. I expected her to go buzzing away but she sat there, staring up at me. On her face there was no smile, no real expression I could put a name to. She was looking at me the way women do when they're looking inside of you. I moved closer.

"Are you going to your friend's café?" she asked.

"I guess not."

"Going home?"

"I guess so."

She deftly revved the engine.

"In that case, you know what I'd really like?"

"What?"

"That omelet you promised me."

That deep look was still in her eyes, locked on mine. She shifted into gear.

"Well?" she asked.

"Well, hell yes."

"I'll be down after I've showered." The clutch pedal came out and away she went. I wasn't far behind.

When next I saw her she was a different picture and even a different A.J. It started with her pounding on my front door. I opened it and there she stood, hair up in a towel, face scrubbed clean. She was wearing silky gray slacks and blouse and fuzzy slippers.

"You'll wake the tenants!" I laughed.

Her eyes were not only righteous, but cheerful. "No daughter of Molly Egan's ever went sneaking into a man's house after midnight. She always told us to go boldly or don't go. Now what about that omelet?"

"How many like you did Molly Egan have?"

"There's six of us. All girls," she answered, and pushed past me on the way to the kitchen.

I'm a fair hand with a spatula so I was pleased when she glanced knowledgeably about the big, airy room.

"What a kitchen!" she exclaimed.

"You ought to see it on a sunny day."

"Who picked out the flowered wallpaper?"

"I did."

She touched the delicate yellow and blue pattern with her fingertips. "It makes the room. Next thing you'll tell me is that you sew."

"Only buttons."

"You do cook, though?"

Her glance fell meaningfully on the stove top. I said "oops" and slid the skillet from the burner.

She poked around and found plates and silver for the table, an old wooden one I'd painted a glossy white. I cut stacks of buttered toast in half and put a little pot of basswood honey on the table.

"It's late for coffee," she said.

"I made tea."

"It's late for tea."

"I know."

"Well, just a cup."

She squared away to her meal like a country girl

When she'd put away everything in sight, she padded over to my refrigerator, and after poking around inside returned with an orange. She began slicing it to share with me.

"I can go out and get some more groceries if you're still hungry."

Her eyes danced. "Listen, if you'd invited me to dinner you'd have a right to stand on ceremony. But you've got me here for breakfast so you're going to have to expect me to be relaxed."

I glanced down at her hands, resting quietly on the tabletop. Not a tremble in them. My throat tightened.

"You know, A.J.," I began, trying to will my heart back to a normal rhythm, "you fairly take my breath away every time I look at you.

"I wish that didn't sound so much like emphysema. Let's do the dishes."

"I've got a lady who comes in."

"Let's do the dishes anyway."

Standing beside me she dried each plate vigorously, handing a couple of pieces back for rewashing.

"You've got a lady who comes in, huh? I thought this place looked too good for somebody who spends his spare time under antique cars."

"That old Packard doesn't take much to keep up."

"Old Packard, my foot. I've peeked inside that huge workshop. How many cars do you have, anyway?"

"Well, there's the Thunderbird."

"Come off it."

"Not all of them are restored. And some are little more than frames or chassis."

"Never mind," she chuckled. "It's obvious you've got so many you're embarrassed about it."

I led her into the living room. She took the towel off

her head and looked at herself in one of the Spanish gilded mirrors. She used the towel as a brush until she had achieved an approximation of her inverted poppy look.

I slumped onto a fat divan and swung my feet up. She sat in a stuffed chair facing me.

"Thanks for the omelet."

"You're welcome."

She twisted sideways in the chair, her shoulders against one arm and her legs dangling over the other.

"Thanks for the oysters the other day."

"Well, that's the place to go for them."

"Come to think of it, thanks for the apartment. And thanks for finding that bloody bomb."

I stared at her. She was peering up at the ceiling while she talked.

"Hush. You don't owe me any thanks. You're not in my debt."

The violet eyes turned to me. "Yes. You'd say that and you'd mean it."

"It's true. I'll never be able to pay you back for just letting me see you in that little red and black bathing suit of yours."

"You like that, huh?"

"Yeah. I like it."

The eyes went back to the ceiling.

"How long before you're going to throw me out of this place so you can get some sleep?"

The heart again. It must have leapt in my chest. "I was hoping you'd stay all night."

Back came the eyes.

"In this chair?"

Pale light streamed in the floor-to-ceiling windows of

my bedroom. Overhead the fan turned slowly, stirring the soft air and making a gentle pulsing noise each time the armature passed a certain spot.

A.J. stood beside a window, her face and body softly illuminated on one side and in shadow on the other. Her eyes took in the big old country bed and bureaus.

"Nice. It's big and comfortable, like you."

"You're someone special," I said, coming up behind her. "I care about you a lot."

She turned and kissed me ever so softly, her arms slipping up around my neck.

"I know you do," she said. "That's why I've tried to hold back from you. To protect us. With the way I feel, and the way I know you do, we could overwhelm each other. We're both too much what the other one wants."

"And needs."

"Go lie down on the bed," she whispered.

Then slowly, in the dim light, she began to unfasten the mother-of-pearl buttons of her blouse. She left the shirt hanging loosely around her. Shadow and light teased me as she stepped from her slacks and panties. The violet in her eyes was gone but she was looking steadily at me. Finally she let the blouse, her last item of clothing, slip from her shoulders to the floor.

Her bathing suit had not lied. The moonlight ghosted across her body. Lines and curves of shadow faded into delicate planes of muscle and scrubbed skin. She moved toward me. The gray-blue light made oblong sweeps across her hips.

"No," she mouthed as I tried to slip over on the bed and give her room next to me. Her hand pressed my shoulders down against the cool sheet.

She knelt beside me on the bed, her face above mine,

her eyes deep glowing points lost in a silent dark well. As she bent to kiss me, I reached up to touch her sweet-smelling hair and press her to me.

"Lie still," she whispered. "I want to show you how I feel about you."

I felt her move. A knee passed over me and something soft and feathery brushed my stomach. Her hands were on my shoulders. She shifted her weight, and though her hands still pressed against my shoulders, her body was arching longer and inching lower in the bed. We touched and the message was in her eyes. Slowly, tenderly, she flattened against me, easing ever backward. Her eyes no longer looked at mine but at infinity. At last I felt our bodies nested together, firm but delicious. For an instant her eyes darted to mine. Then she laid her head on my chest. Her ear was to my heart. The cool tips of her body lay against my ribs. Her knees clung to my sides. My hands found the curves of her hips, stroked them, and gently, as she wanted, I began to move her against me.

NINETEEN

Breakfast consisted of coffee and grape-nuts. Neither of us was ready for more eggs and neither of us went to the front door for the two papers lying there.

"Did you sleep any, Palmer?"

"Some. You?"

"I don't know. Sleeping, dreaming, awake. They were all the same last night."

"You don't look tired."

"I'm not at all tired."

The violet was back in her eyes. I'd first seen it again while looking down at her at dawn, after she'd learned I wouldn't crush her or hurt her in any way.

"You're right. Your kitchen is even nicer in the sunlight." She propped her chin with a hand. Serenity cloaked her features. For my part I could have sat at that table, looking and remembering, for a long time.

But the telephone rang. It was Moses, asking me to come to the newsroom. When I turned back to A.J. she was on her feet, straightening up.

147

"Don't hurry away," I said.

When she looked at me there was tension in her face and a tremble to her fingers.

"I work in a competitive field. Very competitive. And my number one opponent is a pure devil on a story. I gotta go."

She gathered her things, what few there were, and dashed for the door. There she hesitated and came back. She pulled my head down and kissed me quickly and left. The two papers lying on the doorsill she glanced at, and stepped over. I saw her flying past the cusped arch heading for her apartment. I stooped and picked up the papers but laid them aside.

I showered, dried, and stood before the closet: no guayabera shirt today. Archie Lameroux deserved my best. I took my time and dressed carefully. When I finally pulled the *Tribune* from its plastic bag, time was already pressing me. I glanced over the headlines, leaving the New Seville *Times* on the table. My story looked good. I checked my watch, then hurried out back to the Packard. I usually wasn't this late in the morning.

Or this happy.

Still, it looked like the day we were officially going to say good-bye to Archie Lameroux was going to be gray. There was also a strong wind moving the low clouds. When I walked into the newsroom I couldn't help but stand for a minute by my desk and look around. No jeans. No sweatshirts. I tried to remember the last time every single person who put out the Marlinsport *Tribune* came to work dressed in a suit or a sedate, formal dress. No time came to mind.

"Good story," Paula said, passing by. "We shot it to them this morning."

I nodded and walked over to Moses, who was on the telephone. When he saw me, he motioned for me to wait.

On his desk was another cardboard box of Lameroux's memorabilia he wanted to share with me. Hardly worth a call, I thought unfairly, a little vexed remembering the instant tension the phone's ringing had created in A.J.

But I was wrong to be annoyed. When Moses hung up the phone I could see the anxiety on his face.

"You better see this," he said.

I opened the mildewy lid. Inside, wrapped in a scrap of old newspaper, was a tape. Written in the precise, familiar hand of Archie Lameroux was: "OB. Raiford."

I cocked an eye at Moses. "Have you listened to this?"

"No, I found it this morning in the last load sent over by his sister. I thought you'd want it immediately."

I looked around. There was no good place to settle in the newsroom without facing interruptions. If this tape was what it appeared to be, I was desperate to hear it right away and in private.

Within fifteen minutes I was settled down with a borrowed recorder in one of the seminar rooms at Marlinsport University. The riverside campus, a few blocks from the *Trib*, is built around a century-old hotel of Moorish design, complete with minarets and balconies. I'd found many years ago that there's always a vacant spot in its myriad rooms for a reporter needing privacy. I switched on the recorder.

There was no mistaking that voice. It had a midwestern twang out of place in a southern port town. The old recorder spun out the two voices as though they were in the room with me. The one I hadn't heard in twenty years mingled, startlingly, with that of a man dead four days. I almost expected to hear one voice call me "String Bean" and the other to say in its dry, cracked way, "Palmer, now be exact with these quotes."

In the hallway, summer students passed, talking loudly,

their shoes squeaking on the waxed wood floors. Soon I forgot about them. I was alone with my ghosts.

A.L.: ". . . it on now. Precision is important to me even in interviews not intended for publication."

O.B.: "Print it or not, Grandpa. There's nothing more they can do to me now."

A.L.: "It is perhaps indelicate to thank a man for behaving humanely. Still, I do want to thank you for sparing the child."

O.B.: "Go to hell with your thanks. I read your editorial. I know what you think of me. There wasn't one fuckin' word of gratitude I took the boy to a priest."

A.L.: "I see your point. But kidnapping is a serious offense. And any psychological harm to the boy could last a lifetime."

O.B.: "To hell with that. I treated him good. A lot fairer as a matter of fact than his fuckin' cheapskate grandfather treated me. Why, that little operator probably gained five pounds while I had him."

A.L.: "You evidently fed him sweets and soft drinks."

O.B.: "Yeah. I guess if he'd been thirteen they'd have tacked on five years for ruining his complexion. Shit."

A.L.: "It appears you are not taking your offense as seriously as it is."

O.B.: "Is that so? You really piss me off. I didn't do one fuckin' thing to the kid and what does it get me? Big time in the joint with a bunch of King Kong queers. And you think I don't take it serious. Man, you're as much a sadist as the weirdos in here."

There was the sound of a chair scraping and then footsteps going away and coming back.

O.B.: "All right, Grandpa, get on with it. What do you want with me?"

A.L.: "If it really is so awful in here why don't you tell

150

where the remaining twenty-five thousand dollars is hidden? I'm sure that admission would get you out of prison sooner."

O.B.: "You S.O.B. Every strong-arm and con man doing time in this joint is after me night and day for that money. Now you show up asking the same crappy questions. Leave me the fuck alone."

A.L.: "You need not be so belligerent with me, Mr. Blair. I've made a hard trip up here to talk to you."

O.B. "Yeah, I bet you really suffered. Why didn't you send your errand boy String Bean? I'd rather talk to him anyway."

A.L.: "Why is that?"

O.B.: "Well . . let's see, old man . . . maybe I split the money with him. Ever think of that?"

A.L.: "He's married now to a fine young woman who's got him scrambling to find enough money to make a down payment on a piece of land. I don't think he fits the picture of a conniving opportunist."

O.B.: "He's laying low. Like me. Doesn't want to spend it while you're watching."

A twangy laugh sounded for several seconds.

A.L.: "All this steel and concrete seems to me to be an impediment to any far-ranging enterprise on your part."

O.B.: "Why don't you try English for a change, Grandpa?"

A.L.: "I wish, Mr. Blair, rather than continue jousting with me, that you would consider your position and do something for yourself."

O.B.: "Yeah. Raiford's a great place to do something for yourself."

A.L.: "Perhaps I can help you if you will be forthright with me."

O.B.: "Damn you!"

151

There was the sound of slapping on wood.

O.B.: "I told the fuckin' truth. What more do you want?"

A.L.: "Believe me, I want to try to put this episode to rest, not incur your wrath."

O.B.: "Episode? Episode? Is that what you call this shitty place?"

A.L.: "You put yourself in here. All the profanity in the world won't change that."

O.B.: "Yeah, I took the kid. Fattened him up, you said it yourself. Kept him safe and sound on my little island. I was a dumb fucker trying to squeeze a little traveling money from a peckerhead rich man who'd never miss it. But I didn't touch a hair on the boy's head and you bastards repay that by putting me in Shit City."

A.L.: "I told you we are grateful for David's return. That is why I'm here."

O.B.: "Not if all you want to know is where the fuckin' money is. I told them about that at the trial. I told the cops. I told the press. I told my fuckin' attorney."

A.L.: "You still insist you do not have the money? But it has not turned up."

O.B.: "The cops found all the money I had. Period. But what the fuck, I'm nothing but a lousy criminal, right? You don't believe me. Okay, let's say I return the money. What then?"

A.L.: "If you tell the authorities where the rest of the ransom is, I believe at least half your sentence will be lifted."

O.B.: "You're a mean son of a bitch."

A.L.: "I don't understand."

O.B.: (Mimicking) "I don't understand."

A.L.: "How am I angering you?"

O.B.: "Let's see. I got twenty years to life for the kidnapping and extortion, right?"

A.L.: "That's correct."

O.B.: "If I turn over this twenty-five thousand dollars, I'll get off with ten. Right?"

A.L.: "I'm in no position to bargain with you, but I think there is that possibility."

O.B.: "Okay. If half my sentence is for the kidnapping and the other half is for the money, it means you S.O.B.s value the money and the boy equally. And all this gratitude stuff is so much shit."

A.L.: "That's a leap in logic I can't follow."

O.B.: "Yeah. Well, see if you can follow this. I'm up to here in rich bastards and prison queens probing me for money. If I was as grubby for money as the rest of you assholes, I wouldn't be in here and that kid wouldn't be eating out of a silver spoon again. I'd be in Mexico and he'd be in the bottom of the bay."

A.L.: "You can hardly regret not killing the boy."

There was a long silence in which only the faint sound of hard breathing was audible. And then a bang, what could have been a chair falling.

O.B.: "Guard! Guard! Get me out of here before I beat the hell out of this idiot and get myself another ten years."

There was an audible snap as the tape was turned off. The hallway sounds of the university returned to me. Pigeons milled mindlessly on one of the window ledges as a minaret bulged turniplike into the framed scene.

I sat in the small, humid room a long time, the voices echoing through my brain. Idly I fingered the yellowed scrap of newspaper Lan oux had wrapped around the tape. One side was a hodgepodge of classified ads. The

153

other was a single advertisement by a company long since gone under. It was an ad for delivery trucks. Big ones with metal sides. The prices seemed almost quaint compared to today's. The biggest things they had were selling for $6,895. I replaced the newsprint around the tape just the way I'd found it.

TWENTY

When I finally saw the *Times*'s front page with A.J.'s story on it, Archie Lameroux's inability to communicate with a guy like Owen Blair was immediately driven from my mind. I had room for only one impulse: find A.J. at once.

Phones rang all over Marlinsport before I finally tracked her down in the fire marshal's office.

"Where's your car?"

"In the lot here at Station One. What's the matter?"

"Right now, A.J., have a fireman walk you to your car, then go straight home. I'll meet you there."

"I'm not going to do that! And I can't talk. I'm on the marshal's phone."

"Then I'll come there. Don't leave."

"No. Don't. I'm through here and it's nearly time for Lameroux's funeral anyway. I'll meet you at home."

"A.J., don't be embarrassed and please don't be stubborn. Let a fireman walk you to your car. It's important to me."

"Will you get off the phone if I do?"

"Only if you promise."

"Okay. I'll be there in ten minutes."

When the red VW pulled in, I saw it safely stowed in the garage and led A.J. into the kitchen.

"Palmer Kingston in a three-piece suit and wingtips," she exclaimed, but she was forcing it. There was edginess and worry in every syllable.

I held the *Times* before her. "Where did you get this new picture of Owen Blair?"

A little pride joined the edginess in her face. "Well, I got it. That's enough. You and Salgado and everybody else took your first look at Blair after twenty years in this morning's *Times*."

"We sure as hell did."

"Chief Salgado was tickled to death. He told me so."

"The little chief would do better if he was tickled less and spent more time tracking down this ugly bird."

"Come on, Palmer. Salgado's your friend."

"Yeah, friend. You know I never met Owen Blair face to face. All I'd ever seen of him was once from the back of a courtroom and those old prison mug shots."

"So now you know he's kind of shaggy and has a lot of creases in his face."

"And gray hair and bad teeth and an absolutely wild look."

"I guess I did okay then."

"Goddamnit, A.J. That nasty son of a bitch was standing ten feet behind you at the fire last night. If I hadn't happened along . . ."

A visible tremble shook her body, but she settled quickly and I could see her mind struggling.

"I didn't even know Blair was in town until I read your

story this morning. But the marshal told me the fire was electrical."

"No one ever said Blair was a firebug."

She nodded, black hair bouncing. Something of defiance was building in her. She might be scared, but she damned sure wasn't going to back off anything because of it.

"It could have been coincidence—his being there," she said.

"You wouldn't suggest that if you'd seen the look on his face. He was watching you."

"You're saying he followed me there?"

"Yes. And I think he put the bomb in your car."

She flinched as if I'd hit her, turned away from me, and walked over to stare out the kitchen window.

"I don't want to scare you, but Blair is out to get you."

She swung around, hugging her arms to her body. "But why? These murders are only stories to me. Damned big stories, but I'm not personally involved."

"In some way you are, at least to Owen Blair."

"I haven't exactly done a crackerjack job of investigating these murders," she said. "I've just followed the news."

"And ticked off Owen Blair."

"I don't see it."

"I think I do."

The violet eyes were wide and fearful. She waited.

"Your stories on Delano have all used one paragraph over and over—the standard backgrounder used in running stories."

"You saying I made a mistake?"

"No. But you—or the desk—have been . . . well . . . clumsy is too hard a word . . . maybe you've been underinformed."

157

"Don't pussyfoot."

She looked like a little cadet standing there, still, taking it but defiantly.

"Okay. You always say it the same way: 'Blair never revealed where the rest of the ransom money was hidden. But he was not caught for several days after the child was recovered unharmed.' Right?"

"He *was* recovered unharmed."

"No, he was *released* unharmed. I've just spent an hour listening to a taped interview of Blair made almost twenty years ago at Raiford by Archie Lameroux. Blair was adamant that he'd been treated unfairly by the press."

"A kidnapper treated unfairly? That's standard con talk."

"Blair took the boy to a church and left him sitting in a pew. David was not only unharmed, he was downright cheerful. Treated the whole thing like an adventure. I know. I talked to him. But the newspapers, especially the *Tribune*, howled against Blair and never gave him any credit for taking care of the boy and releasing him. None at all."

"How long's he been in town?" A.J. asked.

"At least a few days. That's all I know."

"Long enough to commit murder?"

"Or long enough to read your stories about the murders, and the kidnapping."

"Which intensified an old grudge?"

"Your newspaper has been slamming him around every day."

"And they're all my stories."

"Right, and regardless if Blair had anything to do with Delano's or Lameroux's murder, he has to be found immediately."

"You shouldn't be telling me this," she said.

I could tell she was already fighting a battle with herself.

"A time comes when beating the competition is not the most important thing," I said slowly. "Sometimes even the First Amendment is not the only consideration."

Her gaze fell to the floor, to her shoes. "Palmer, I don't have the right to tell you anything."

The urge to go to her, to pull her to me was strong, but I knew I couldn't. Instead I tried a little smile.

"I'll tell you then," I said. "You tracked down Blair's girlfriend or a relative in Chicago and got the picture, promising not to reveal its source. But you've got to tell the police so they can protect both of you. Blair's a dangerous man."

She was thinking hard. When she looked up, resolution was in her eyes. "I'm a good reporter. I don't get rattled and I try not to make mistakes. It would be a mistake for me, new on the *Times* staff, to burn a source. But as you say, she might be in danger. I guess I'd better get with my editors."

"They'll tell you to go to the police."

"I know."

"Fine, if that's the way you want it. It's been a long time since I've been to the *Times* bureau."

"What do you mean?" she asked.

"I'm going to follow you. Once you walk through that door I'm going to feel a lot better."

TWENTY-ONE

After Archie Lameroux's austere funeral—which he'd insisted on in a document left with his sister—I cruised in gloomy splendor to the newspaper. The Packard gleamed like a waxed banana. I eased it to the curb across from the guard station.

A large green and white Jones rental truck, backed up to the loading dock, was taking on a few tons of waste newsprint for recycling. Newspapers have more ways to cut costs and make money out of nothing than any business I know. That the *Tribune*, with a huge fleet of its own, would rent trucks for its twice-a-week peak delivery days proved it.

"Move that jalopy out of the way," a harsh voice called from the truck. The sour-faced old driver leaned out, waving at me. He was too far away for me to make out the tattoo on his withered biceps, but I didn't care anyway.

"You've got plenty of room," I said, closing the Packard door behind me. "There's enough space to maneuver an L-ten-eleven out of there."

160

He grumbled under his breath and gunned the truck's engine as I passed.

I sprinted up the stairs. It was payday and most everybody who'd been at the funeral was back and no doubt had collected their reward for a week of newspapering. At Wilson's secretary's desk I picked up my envelope and signed the computer printout sheet where I, as well as a lot of others in the newsroom, lied about putting in only forty hours last week.

Wanting privacy, I went into the interview room and grabbed a phone.

A.J., I found, was on the way to New Seville to confer with higher editors. That was okay. The *Times* would surely call Salgado and get her protection.

As I emerged from the little room Moses called me over. "Which of these do you like better?" he asked.

On his screen were two lead paragraphs for the Lameroux funeral story. I was touched by his asking my opinion.

"They're both good."

"Which one's better?"

I put a hand on his bony shoulder. "That's for you to decide. I'm not about to give writing advice to Moses Johnson."

He gave me an exasperated look and turned back to his terminal.

Wilson came out and scanned the newsroom. He called loud enough for everyone in the newsroom to hear: "Hey, Paula. Any way we can get a recent photo of Owen Blair? I see the *Times* got one."

The smartass. I kept on walking.

Downstairs Smitty was coming on duty. As I passed the guard station, I nodded and got a frown in return. I wondered about that for the split second it took me to reach the

161

glass doors. There I came to a stop. My eyes were riveted on the Packard.

"Sure is a shame, Palmer."

All I could do was stare out the door at my twelve-cylinder, pale yellow, double-waxed, beautifully chromed 1935 model 1208 convertible—the one with the ugly scrape along the left front fender. The one with its heavy steel bumper bent forward.

It wasn't like somebody shot Bambi, I know that. Any car is only metal and rubber and other parts. But, my God, that Packard was half a century old!

"Can't stand to look at it, and can't stand to look away. Right?" Smitty asked, coming over beside me. "I know the feeling. My father had a Packard once."

I still didn't speak.

"You might as well go on out there and get it over with. It's not that bad. Course you'll never match the color. The whole car will have to be repainted."

I turned slowly from the door.

"I take it no one left word about scraping my car."

"Nope."

"Where's the Jones Trucking office?"

He fumbled through the phone book.

"Office is over in the Stoneman Building. Doesn't say where the trucks are kept."

"Who'd know?"

"Around here? Mr. Gibbons. Our comptroller."

"Why not circulation?"

He shrugged. "Circulation wants trucks, they always see Mr. Gibbons."

"Then I guess I will, too." I started back toward the stairs.

Smitty called after me. "Driving for Jones is only one notch above selling blood. They see a hoss like you and they'll all run hide."

At the top of the stairs I stalked past data processing and classified before reaching the big double doors to the business office.

Reggie Gibbons stocks his department the same way a Japanese lord stocks his fish pond—with a critical eye for color and form. Only for Reggie the color tends to honey blond and the form is voluptuous. There may have been two or three men in there, for appearances' sake, but nobody ever notices. All you ever see is peekaboo blouses and tight skirts. The women in the newsroom resent the hell out of it but they can never get any of the women Reggie hires to care.

"Well, hello, Palmer!" chirped Adel Nottles, Reggie's secretary. "I'm surprised you found your way in here. It's been so long."

I tried to keep my attention lifted to her big blue eyes but it was a struggle and she knew it.

"Can I see Reggie?"

She stood, a little huffily, and ducked her head in his office. Reggie looked up through the half-glass panels and motioned me to come in. As I sidled past, Adel murmured, "I heard you had a nice party Saturday night."

Reggie's booming welcome saved me from having to answer.

I closed the door behind me.

"The till's empty," he joked. "Don't come to me looking for cash."

His laugh was wet and sticky. Gibbons was in his early thirties, a hot accountant searching for a way up. He was never going to find it and no one was ever going to tell him that his addiction to chewing gum was all that stood in his way.

I asked for the address of Jones's lot and told him about the damage to the Packard. He consulted a file.

"Make 'em pay up," he said, handing over the address. "They can afford it."

"Well, it happened on private property, I was in a no-parking zone, and so far I don't have a witness. That may figure against me."

"If they give you any trouble, let me know," Gibbons said. "Those birds have had a sweetheart deal around here for so long a little prod in the ass would be therapeutic."

"I thought your job was to correct things like that."

"I could do better than Jones, but Jones it's been for some twenty years. Hammersmith won't hear of a change."

He chomped away on his gum like a beaver on a birch tree. "Going to that lot's not going to do you any good. The dispatcher can't cut a check."

"Yeah, but I want to see the truck, and the driver."

On the way out I passed Adel with a weak nod. My mind was still on the car, but not so much that I couldn't feel those hard blue eyes on my back.

Two turns around the Packard satisfied me the damage was limited to the left front. I climbed aboard and eased my battered classic into the street.

The crowded lot on the edge of Alverez District was a potholed, ungraded corner with a dispatcher's shack and an old metal maintenance shed. There was no one outside. I found the truck I was looking for parked close to the padlocked shed. Paint from the Packard was on its front bumper and it was still loaded with old newsprint. I wrote down the truck's number.

Through dirty glass I peered into the dispatcher's grungy room. The sour-faced old driver was gesturing and talking to a second man I figured was the dispatcher. I stepped inside.

"Telling him about your bad driving?"

"Who are you?" the man barked, twirling in his squeaky chair to face me. A cigarette hung from his mouth.

"I'm the guy with the banged-up car and the bad temper," I said.

"I didn't do nothin'!" the driver grunted, crossing his tattooed arms in front of his chest.

"The paint's still on the bumper of your truck."

"Shit, man, I asked you to move."

"You'd have to be blind to clip me." I turned to the dispatcher. "You sent a man straight off the streets to the *Trib*?"

"What do you want?" he asked. "An apology? Him? My job? What?"

"No. A paint job."

He shrugged. "You're wasting your time here. All I do is keep the trucks rolling."

"Don't let that truck roll or Jones Trucking may have to bail you and your driver out of jail. I'm calling the police."

"Hey, hold on a minute," the dispatcher said, dialing the telephone. "If what you want is a paint job, let me talk to the office."

"No, let me talk to them." I held out my hand. He gave up the receiver and the truck driver went out, closing the door very carefully behind him.

The soft feminine voice that announced "Jones Trucking" in my ear sounded vaguely familiar. I quickly told her what was up.

165

"You're Palmer Kingston?" she asked.

"Yes."

"Hold on a moment, please."

After a short wait she came back on the line and ever so nicely told me Jones Trucking regretted the incident and would pay to have the Packard painted.

"It's going to involve more than touching up a fender," I explained, disbelieving. "The entire car will have to be repainted, the bumper needs work, and it's going to take a specialist. I don't let just anyone touch my Packard."

"It's all right, Mr. Kingston," she assured me. "You get the car fixed and send the bill to Jones Trucking. If the repair man needs confirmation of this, have him contact us at the Stoneman Building. You have our number?"

"Yes," I replied.

"And this will satisfy you?"

"Sure," I said, and wondering why I still felt suspicious added, "thanks."

The dispatcher was smiling. "See, buddy," he soothed, "no need to get hot over a little thing like a car bump."

I nodded absently on my way out the door. I cranked up my carriage and crept toward home. It was with relief that I at last nosed the Packard deep into its slot and draped a cloth over the fender.

Once I'd taken a quick shower and changed, I called the *Times* Building but couldn't locate A.J.

My guess was she was at Salgado's office. I thought I'd take a ride over there myself.

The Jeep balked and then came to life. A stop by the Stoneman Building wouldn't hurt since it was right on the way.

The lobby was empty. Only the echo of my footsteps on the tile greeted me. The directory listed Jones Trucking

166

on the fifth floor, below Artie Brent's office. The brass cage-work rattled all the way up and a shiver ran through the metal. I'm mechanic enough to recognize the effects of excessive play from worn parts. Still, I understand why Artie doesn't drop the old beast of a building inside its own walls and raise one of those glass ice cubes that attract lawyers and bankers with more money than taste. I smiled to myself. Like me, the old manipulator had a feeling for the past.

The fifth floor was the same as all the others in the Stoneman. There was a core of elevators and restrooms with a corridor running around it like a square doughnut. On the outside were the offices, which once looked down on other Marlinsport buildings. Now they look up.

Jones Trucking was stenciled in small black letters along the bottom of a frosted glass door. It was locked. There were no office hours posted and no telephone number to call in case of an emergency. The mail slot was sealed.

Beneath my feet the doorsill was a bar of granite, white with blue veins, and worn down by the commerce of the ages. I dropped to my knees, laid my head flat against the gritty floor, and tried to peek inside.

"What are you doing down there?" a puzzled voice inquired from behind me. I scrambled, red-faced, to my feet. A short but large woman with a cleaning cart gazed at me with more interest than displeasure.

" 'Scuse me. I have some business with Jones Trucking and I'm trying to figure out how to get in touch with them."

"Well, it really must be some business for you to put your head down there on that old floor. You've got grit in your hair and dirt on your pants."

I brushed vigorously.

"Do they always go home at four?" I asked.

"Go home at four?" She laughed and began rummaging through a pocket bulging with keys. She found the one she wanted and inserted it into the door, loose in its frame after all these years. It swung open easily.

"Honey, they stay at home."

The office was empty. Not only were there no people, but nothing else, either. No furniture, no telephones, no carpets, no files. Only bare dirty walls and black wood floors.

"When did they move out?" I asked. Rubbing my finger along a low wooden partition I found thick dust.

The woman frowned. "That's not my fault," she declared. "I'm not supposed to touch this place."

"Does Jones have another office in the building?"

"They don't even have this one, do they?" she responded, then added, "There's stuff stored in the next room."

She opened a door to reveal stacks of folding chairs, an artificial Christmas tree, and boxes of broken fixtures. It appeared to be the storage area for the whole building.

"So when did you stop cleaning in here?"

"Stop? I never started. That's why I laughed when you said you wanted to see them. There's no them."

"What about the company's mail? The phones?" I pointed to the name on the door. "This is a real company, not a confidence game."

Her eyes danced. "I don't know about that, but they sure do seem to have one great big fish on their hook."

She scooted me out of the office ahead of her and locked the door.

Instead of waiting for the slow elevator, I made for the stairwell. I was only going up one floor, not down five. But my walk was for nothing. Artic Brent's office was closed, too. Whatever he knew about his strange tenant on the fifth floor would have to keep until tomorrow. This time I waited for the creaky elevator. It took forever.

TWENTY-TWO

Tension crackled in Paula's voice as I lifted the jangling pressroom telephone from its cradle at police headquarters.

"Palmer? That you?"

When I said it was, I heard her call to someone, "It's okay. I've got him on the phone now." Then to me: "Have you seen Walter Hammersmith?"

"Sure. He gave that disjointed talk at graveside. You were there."

"No. Since then."

I pondered. Did I last see him getting in his car at Lameroux's funeral, or was that Delano's? There'd been too many funerals lately.

"I saw Walter leave in a hurry with his wife. He didn't look good. My guess is he's drinking somewhere."

"Damn. He had appointments this afternoon with some of the chain's top executives. He wouldn't get sloshed and forget a group like that, would he? Even over Archie Lameroux?"

170

"You try Walter's home?"

"No answer. Christ, these guys flew all the way from Washington for the funeral. Tonight they've got reservations at Luxor's Steak House with Hammersmith."

"That's what those corporate guys came to Marlinsport for. To eat at Luxor's and get laid at Elsa's. They never even knew Lameroux."

"I don't give a shit what they came for. I don't want them leaving disappointed or pissed off, either one."

"So you want me to see if I can find Walter."

"You'll be doing him a favor, you know. Call me soon, will you?"

"Okay, Paula."

As I hung up, a frazzled A.J. walked in.

"Snitching stinks," she sighed and slumped down on one of the icy steel chairs. She got right back up.

"Been sitting too long," she said sharply, tension in her every movement as she leaned over the table and stared at me. Her fingers made a drumbeat on the metal top. "How was the funeral?"

"Rough. Hammersmith was almost incoherent and Chastain, surrounded by his bodyguards, went on and on, reciting what he called the glory days of the *Tribune*. I bet Wilson hated it."

"What do you mean?"

"Well, Chastain didn't compare the end of the Lameroux era with the decline of the Roman Empire but there was no problem in seeing what he meant."

"Did he say anything about the kidnapping?"

"Oh, yes. He talked about Lameroux's part in freeing his grandson and repeated the story of Delano's wild ride to exchange the ransom. He even mentioned me."

"I should have been there."

I met her eyes. "How'd things go with your source?"

"Okay. I called her before I contacted Salgado." She hesitated, then added, "She lives in Marlinsport. It took awhile but I finally convinced her to talk to the chief. But she doesn't know where Blair is and she's mad at me."

I reached out and touched A.J.'s nervous hand.

"You did the woman a big favor. If she was dumb enough to give you Blair's picture and not expect him to know where it came from, then she's too dumb to get out of this mess without help."

"Watch who you call dumb. I feel kinda sleazy for manipulating her in the first place."

"I bet she called you."

"Yes." She sounded surprised.

"For some purpose of her own you probably still haven't figured out."

"What do you think?"

I shrugged. "A lover's quarrel?"

"She had a bandaged arm," A. J. said tensely. "But she never indicated Blair was back in town. Just that she had this photo taken after he got out of Raiford a year or so ago."

"You thinking he could have been staying with her off and on?"

Her answer was slow in coming and I was suddenly afraid she'd think I was pressing her for information.

"Forget I asked," I said.

She smiled. "It's okay. I just realized you're probably right."

"You got a story to write?" I asked, picking up the telephone.

"No. Since someone else covered the funeral, I'm through for the day."

"Give me a few minutes," I whispered with my hand over the mouthpiece.

"What's wrong?" A.J. asked.

"Oh, our publisher's off somewhere dealing with his feelings after the funeral, and the newspaper wants him. The problem is he doesn't seem to want to be found right now."

I made a number of calls under A.J.'s interested gaze. Finally the bartender at the Rocking Horse told me Walter stopped in the club early in the afternoon, had two martinis, and left as quietly as he'd arrived. Two drinks would barely get him started, I thought as I tried another bar. In a city still as small-townish as Marlinsport, it's a tough job to lose a publisher, especially one like Walter. He usually wants to be seen and often stops at more than one place to do his drinking. Only this time it didn't work out. Nobody'd seen him after he left the Rocking Horse.

"Do you have to find him?" A.J. asked as I hung up after a half dozen more tries.

"They were hoping I could, but I'm stumped."

"If you're finished, why don't we pick up some supper to eat by the pool? Your publisher is not the only one who'd like to get away."

Her eyes were tired, but there was a spark back in there, very deep.

"We could go by Spanish Village," I said. "They'd fix us a basket with sandwiches and cheese and a little wine . . ."

The glimmer in her eyes was growing. I felt my own spirits lifting from watching her, but my brain was still struggling with where Walter Hammersmith could be. He wasn't the kind to miss an appointment with his superiors.

"You going to wear that little red and black swimming suit?" I asked.

"We'll see." She grinned.

The telephone rang. It was Paula.

"Any luck?"

"No."

"Damn." I heard her breathing. "Well, let it go. I don't know why I should worry about him anyway. Wilson'll be glad to meet with these guys."

She hung up, satisfied the crisis was past.

I wished I were that sure. When I glanced up, tiredness was closing in around the fading light in A.J.'s eyes.

"You going back to work?" she asked.

"I ought to."

"Probably just as well," she yawned.

I stood up. "Has a cop been assigned to you yet?"

"No cops. I'll be fine in that little fortress of mine. And I can get home by myself."

We walked to our cars. When it became obvious to A.J. that I was following her, she motioned me away a couple of times, but I just waved back. Finally she gave up.

Back at the apartments, despite her protests, I escorted her up the stairs. I checked each room thoroughly, making A.J. laugh when I peered under the bed. She took my arm, pulled me to my feet, and pushed me toward the door, where I got a quick smack on the lips and a quicker good-bye. I listened to the bolt slide in place.

As I drove out the back gate, I waved to the cop in the unmarked police car parked down the street. Good old Salgado.

TWENTY-THREE

Spacious lawns with precise landscaping rolled past as I lead-footed the Jeep south on Bay Drive. Old money soon gave way to new in the shape of tedious high rises, replacements for other stately homes that I still remembered. I zipped past Bay Court, half expecting to see Archie Lameroux stroll out, and then quickly approached the Columns restaurant, midway point on the parklike drive between the university at its northern end and the Yacht Club to the south.

A long peach-colored sunset was beginning as I swung through the gate of the boatyard and stopped at the guard station.

"I'm looking for Mr. Walter Hammersmith," I said as I signed the visitor's book.

"The Commodore? He's not here, at least on this side," the guard said. "He sometimes parks in the other lot. You know, for dinner or parties."

"Could he reach his boat from over there?"

"Oh, sure."

"I'll take a look then."

I was pointed toward a row of masts and fishing towers.

They do it right at the Yacht Club. There's no crisscrossing of hoses and extension cords over the docks the way you see at most marinas. Here slant-topped chests are stocked at each berth, with the boat's name stenciled on. And at the head of each dock is a white cart mounted on bicycle wheels, ready to carry tackle or machines or a couple or three cases of liquor and ice out to the waiting craft.

Boats are berthed at MYC in three distinct classes: money, lots of money, and beyond money. Walter's boat was at one of the middle docks, a respectable distance from either extreme. I parked and strolled over.

His yacht, the *Mil Line Rater*, looked to be about sixty feet long. With white Fiberglas hull and teak decking, she was more party boat than anything else, although in a pinch you could fish from the stern. Walter had gone for power, not style. The only canvas in sight was a little scrap over the flying bridge and an awning over the rear deck. This big beast would gulp petroleum like a tugboat.

"Hello!" I called. Except for a light in a smaller fishing boat in the next berth, the dock was dark and deserted in the twilight. No answer came from Walter's boat, but I stepped aboard anyway. It was so large it hardly rocked. A gentle swell lapped at the hull: plop . . . plop.

The cabin opened to a touch, although there was a high-quality lock built into it. I stuck my head in and called Walter's name, then backed out and mounted the teak and chrome steps to the flying bridge. A canvas rain cover for the skipper's seat was tossed next to an empty holder for a small fire extinguisher under the control panel. I sank into the chair and surveyed the yacht basin from my lofty perch. There must have been a couple of hundred boats in sight. Millions and millions of dollars worth of toys. No stretch of the imagination could have turned this barge of Walter's into something practical. I was honestly a little disgusted by the thing. A wide shelf intended for the storage and spreading of charts instead held decks of bridge cards, a tumbler with the boat's name in gold on it and an ounce of Scotch still in the bottom, a black formal bowtie, an opened can of pistachios, and a folded cocktail pennant that would draw Walter's peer group like ants when he hoisted it.

"Well, Palmer, are you early for an appointment or do you intend to steal the man's boat?"

Even big guys jump when they're startled. Artie Brent laughed at me from the offshore fisherman next door.

"Don't tell me Marlinsport's most famous crusader has a guilty conscience like everybody else? You almost fell overboard there."

"Even Saint Peter checks over his shoulder when the Devil's dogging him. I'm looking for Walter."

"He's been known to sleep one off in there. Security should have a key."

"It's open."

"That so?" He sounded surprised.

"Yeah. I tried it."

"That's more trust than I ever imagined Walter Hammersmith would put in his fellow man. You check for him below?"

"I called out."

"That's for sure. I heard you. But if he's really been sucking up martinis you couldn't wake him with a hundred-piece band. Let's have a look."

177

Artie scrambled across the dock and dropped onto the rear deck. He looked at the keyhole, shrugged, then pushed open the door. A good-sized lounge with plenty of glass and stuffed furniture gave way to a galley stocked largely with the paraphernalia of those on liquid diets.

"This is his cabin," Artie said, and opened a door that revealed a well-made double bunk.

"Not here. How about the other." He took a few steps, stuck his head in a second cabin, also empty.

Back in the galley, he pulled a long cigar from his pocket, peeled it, opened one of three doors under the sink, and dropped the cellophane in a trash can.

"Always best to be tidy on the other fellow's boat," he said.

Using a gold lighter, he fired up.

"How's the family?" I asked.

"Which one?"

"Marta."

"She's smoking too much."

"If your house smells like that thing in your mouth, I guess she has to smoke for self-defense."

He laughed. "Maybe you're right."

I swept my hand over the orderly luxury of Walter's cabin. "I know you got money to spare for that dinghy of yours, but I'd really not stopped to consider that being a publisher had so many rewards."

Artie studied the damp end of his cigar. "You know, Palmer, I've heard the same kind of statement about you and that palace you call home."

"That's an apartment building."

"Sure," he replied sarcastically. "But you and I both know it doesn't have to be. I've also seen the documentary stamps on the land transfer of that little farm you used to own."

"Nosing around, huh?"

"Palmer, you've been coming to me for years because I know stuff. Of course I'm going to know about you, too."

"You do keep informed, I give you that." I leaned back against the bar. "Tell me, do you keep as close a watch on your tenants?"

"Close enough not to let them get more than a month behind on their rent. Why?"

"I've got some personal business with Jones Trucking."

He smiled, waiting.

"You know they haul newsprint to the *Tribune?*" I asked. "Even make delivery runs."

"So?"

"So one of their trucks hit my car at the *Trib.* It's going to cost a lot to get it fixed."

"Jones will pay for it."

"You seem awful sure."

"Palmer. I know how you are about ethics. You don't want to use your position to gain any personal advantages for yourself."

"That's right."

"Well, you don't have to worry about using your name to put pressure on Jones. There's no way on God's earth that trucking firm will risk its relationship with the *Tribune* over a scraped fender and a bent bumper."

"The paint job's going to cost."

A great cloud of cigar smoke wreathed his head. "They'll pay."

"Yeah. Well, I won't have to seize all their furnishings then. Tell me, Artie, what's that empty office about? They got some kind of tax dodge?"

The glitter in his eyes wasn't quite as friendly as it had been a moment before. Apparently he wasn't happy with the revelation that I'd been snooping around his building.

"There's nothing illegal about Jones Trucking. You'll get your money to fix the Packard."

The truth dawned on me then, late but full-grown. He already knew about the accident. I hadn't mentioned the Packard. Or how it was damaged. And now I'd recognized the telephone voice at Jones Trucking. It belonged to Artie's secretary.

"You're a partner in Jones Trucking, aren't you?"

He pulled on his cigar without comment, or any indication he ever would have one.

"Tonight I want Walter Hammersmith, and that's all," I said, straightening. "Can you help me?"

He spread his hands in a gesture of regret.

I left him and sped north on Bay Boulevard.

Worry about Walter whirled around my brain. I turned up the volume on the police scanner under the dash. The tiny red lights flickered in a wave from left to right, pausing for an instant or longer as squad cars and detectives, rescue vehicles and ambulances, as well as *Trib* reporters and photographers, communicated with their dispatchers. No mention of Hammersmith. It was time to let the police in on his disappearance, but it wasn't my place to do it.

An idea crossed my mind like an icicle. Paula and I were contacting Hammersmith's haunts. But if the worst was true—the image of Archie Lameroux's pathetic body on the Banana Docks came to mind—Hammersmith's hangouts didn't really matter. Owen Blair's secret lair was the key.

I stopped at a phone booth and called Paula.

"Palmer, it's not going to look good if Hammersmith's

holed up somewhere drinking. Once we call the police it's public." Her words came carefully. "It might take me awhile to reach Wilson and clear this."

"To hell with Wilson. Call Salgado and tell him everything we know."

"We don't know anything."

"The *Trib*'s got a murdered editor and a missing publisher. We can be forgiven a little hysteria."

"I'm not hysterical."

"Well, I'm getting mighty close. Will you call or shall I?"

One of Paula's virtues is her ability to adapt quickly to an altered situation.

"I'll call, but you keep hunting him on your own. Okay?"

"Okay."

As I headed for the Jeep a fresh breeze picked up with a temperature change I didn't like. Pinhead-size bursts of rain touched my face, almost stinging, dropping not from the distant skies but squeezed by the falling degrees in the very air itself. Such rosettes of water are the harbingers of mighty storms. Distant thunder rolled in from the west.

When the open police channel came on with the APB on Walter I felt a little better. I'd have felt a lot better if I thought they knew any more than I did about where to look.

Where would the paths of Walter Hammersmith and Owen Blair cross? One answer, of course, was Archie Lameroux's funeral. The old editor might have brought those two together.

TWENTY-FOUR

I headed toward the cemetery. The storm was sweeping northeastward and coming fast. I found myself unconsciously pressing the accelerator to the floor. On the slope of graves, Spanish moss swayed and danced in the ancient oaks. Leaves also were beginning to break loose and scatter before the rising wind. Archie Lameroux's wreaths tipped in the newly turned earth and flower petals studded the trembling grass.

Owen Blair could have stood behind hedges or in the copse or behind the rows of crypts. If he did manage to hang around without being seen, and if he was as angry over his years in prison as I believed, he could have snatched Walter. But when? Certainly not at the cemetery. I saw Walter and his wife drive off in their tan Cadillac.

The Jeep scattered gravel as I gunned out of the cemetery. I should have wandered around the area during Lameroux's services. But saying good-bye had been important to me, too.

One raindrop the size of a marble landed on the wind

shield. There was a sizzling lightning strike followed by a clap of thunder like a railroad locomotive had been dropped on my roof. Then came the rain. Jesus, did it rain. The news staff was going to be working a second big story tonight. The rain was only starting and already I knew where the storm sewers would back up, which intersections would be under water, which low neighborhoods would be flooded out. Marlinsport can't take a big rain. The city may have tripled its expanses of asphalt, high rises, and houses in the last ten years, but its drainage remained essentially the same. When the two or three deluges come every summer, there's always a big commotion for a day or two about what has to be done and then, when the carpets dry out, everyone seems to forget.

I popped into four-wheel drive as I crept through the outskirts. The wipers fought a useless battle. Opposing forces pulled at the Jeep as the elements pounded from one side while runoff guzzling into sewers tugged in another direction. Streetlights flared on and flickered off as lightning bit into the circuits. My headlamps created short cones filled with shimmering streaks that could pass for icicles hanging on a Christmas tree. I didn't slow as I sloshed up to Walter's pillared home in the Establishment's part of town. There were lights on, and I felt a pang for his wife. He was a hard man, driven and relentless, and I doubted he'd ever had much time for her.

She came to the door quickly. Lean and tanned, with the look of a woman who took care of herself, she spoiled the effect with an excess of rings and bangles. I learned Walter had dropped her off after the funeral and she'd been at a neighbor's the rest of the afternoon. Her advice to me was to try Walter's boat.

There was nothing else for me to do except follow his

route from home to the Rocking Horse. The bar was the last place he'd been seen. Maybe the bartender could come up with something else.

Relentless rain pounded my canvas roof as I pulled into the parking lot by the bar. It was almost full dark. I sat in the Jeep, engine idling, trying to gauge if I should wait a few minutes and hope for a break in the deluge. I wiped the fog off the windshield and pressed my head forward to see better. Huge raindrops danced on the hood. On the other side of the lot was a dim light from the interior of a car. The driver's door was ajar, rain pouring inside a brand-new tan Cadillac. Just like Walter Hammersmith's.

I pulled on the yellow slicker and boots always stashed in the back. Wind tore at the Jeep door and water crashed against the seats and paneling in the brief moment it took me to slam it.

The rear bumper of the Cadillac bore a reflective medallion, one coveted at the *Trib*. It was to the executive parking lot. As I slushed forward, a badge in the back window for the Yacht Club caught my eye. This was Walter's car without a doubt. I stuck my head inside. The seats were drenched with water, and high on the driver's seat by something more. Blood by the gruesome look of it.

My adrenaline pumping, I shut the door and ran into the Rocking Horse. Its canvas awning thumped wildly overhead.

The young bartender paled when he heard my news. His hand was shaking as he called the police, meanwhile insisting to me that Walter had left hours before and seemed fine.

"Wasn't he upset?" I demanded.

"Yes! But my God, he was *alive*."

The police came like a shot, crisp carloads of them

184

that wilted instant in the whipcords of rain. But all their paraphernalia and rapid-fire questions got them no more information than I already had. When Randy Holliman arrived, I left it in his hands.

I wasn't sure where I was going as I forced the Jeep back into the flooded streets.

What made me decide to replay a twenty-year-old kidnapping I cannot say. Maybe it was desperation, maybe it was the pounding storm closing me in the small sanctuary of the Jeep with all my thoughts of Owen going back to that other tense and dangerous time.

Almost alone on the streets, I drove once more to the bay, where the wind was bringing briny whitecaps crashing over the parapet. The flash of palm fronds crossed my headlights as they sailed through the rain like ribboned lances.

Owen Blair had picked up little David Chastain at his school because that's where he was vulnerable, just as Walter was vulnerable at the Rocking Horse. And when the first drama began, I played a minor part and that none too successfully. This time I was going to have to do better.

It was a strange obsession that haunted me, coming from some deep reservoir I didn't know I had, more a thing of intuitiveness than logic. Yet, there it was: replay the kidnapping.

Sheets of rotting plywood covered the arched windows of Union Station, where trains no longer screeched into own. I parked as close as I could, ignoring the NO TRES-PASSING signs. Glass glittered on the sidewalk and crunched under my boots. I walked slowly along the wall and fence bordering the station. I knew there had to be a way in because I knew what was inside. It took only a few minutes to find a passage. One track's gate bulged open, obviously forced far enough to allow a normal-size man to squeeze through. But not me. I dragged a broken baggage cart to the fence and, after shedding my slicker and boots, vaulted over.

I raced to the covered walkway. There, taking a deep breath, my stomach turned. Even the driving rain could not cleanse the air of the reek of wine and urine, which intensified sharply when I pushed through the broken waiting-room doors.

Across the room a cluster of candles stood in a paraffin puddle on the ticket agent's counter. They illuminated a ghostly scene suited to Victorian London, if anywhere on earth. There must have been twenty men, maybe even thirty, in the cavernous chamber, huddled on the floor and crawling around like roaches. Maybe a few of them belonged in mental institutions. The majority were soulless drunks from all over the East Coast of America who migrated toward the mythical place where no bed is ever cold.

I switched on my K-lite. Methodically I moved the beam from face to face, looking for Owen, almost afraid to find Walter.

A pair who'd been thrashing about grumbled a warning to me. Others murmured incoherent agreement. I shined the light full on the two and waded roughly toward them in the middle of the room. They swarmed away—all of them—the way ripples run from a rock dropped into a pond. I shined my light around the circle. The fear in their eyes was ludicrous.

"Do any of you know a man named Owen Blair?" I asked.

Silence. I moved toward the pair who'd first grumbled

at me. They squeezed back against the wall, behind others with wide, staring eyes.

"Owen Blair," I repeated.

"For God's sake tell him," squeaked a voice.

Murmurs came, garbled, inarticulate but negative.

"Walter Hammersmith." My light stabbed from face to face. They were even afraid to put up their hands. This time they kept their silence.

I returned to the doors and pushed my way outside to the relatively pure air. This was not the place to find a trail to Walter Hammersmith.

On the other side of the gate a latecomer was fingering my slicker. He'd already tossed aside my big boots as useless to him. The slicker was another matter.

All I said was "Put those boots back," but it was too much.

He started to run with the slicker at the same time his head pivoted to get a look at me. Then he laid down my slicker, returned my boots, and hauled himself out of there as fast as rubber legs could carry him.

I jumped at the bars and huffed and puffed my way over them. The dumb bastard could have taken the stuff and been halfway across the bay by the time I made it over the fence.

Reclad in my rain gear, I plunged back toward the Jeep. A fire-engine siren echoed far away. It was going to be a rough night for a lot of folks, I feared. I let more water inside as I fell into the seat. I was miserable. The floor of the Jeep was slimy with mud and my feet were sloshing around inside the boots. Maybe what I'm doing is madness, I thought.

I weaved my way down flooded streets to the main

dock area. After driving back and forth on the bridges there a couple of times, I at last realized that the phone booth from which I'd talked to Owen years before was gone, taken by a road realignment.

The wind was easing. Maybe the worst of the storm was over. I turned up the scanner. There was no news of Walter.

TWENTY-FIVE

As I eased down the side street in Ballast Anchorage, where Delano and David's father began their long-ago ordeal to drop the ransom money, the windshield wipers flicked softly, knocking away a drop or two at each slow swipe. The idling engine was almost quiet as I glided to a stop. Above the bay, stars were filling the heavens.

I was wary of the old fire escape, but I jumped, catching the bottom step. The ironwork was frozen but two hundred fifteen pounds swinging on the end of a lever will work wonders. The fire escape screamed and the stairs came down.

When I reached the top, I found the roof was caved in and the parapet leaning in places. It would be death to walk up there. I went back down.

The moon came out bright and full. I crossed the glistening street and entered the desolation of Mendez Bakery. Surprised, circumspect eyes in the piles of trash glittered back at me. I let the rats return to their scavenging and hurried out. My eyes studied each nearby building, searching for movement or a beam of light. I'd run out of places to go. The island where Owen Blair had held David Chastain would require a boat to check and I was sure Salgado had already covered that.

There was the park—where the ransom was finally dropped. One of the most frequented places in Marlinsport now, it no longer had deep brush or dark corners. Owen would have taken Walter—if he hadn't already killed him—to a secret place, Owen's kind of place, seedy, lonely, and . . . a sudden thought . . . maybe where he could watch the struggles of those he'd bested, the way he'd watched and mocked me so long ago.

My gaze drifted to the left, remembering the night the car with Delano crept around the corner, heading for this spot. Inside the bakery they'd picked up the note. My eyes traveled to the parapet across the street. From there I'd watched them read it in the car headlights. And I in turn had been watched by the FBI.

To the right, the dark car had swung in, idling, full of plainclothesmen, watching, too. If Owen Blair also watched that drama two decades before, he hadn't watched it from inside the box created by me, Delano, the cops behind me, or the ones parked to either side of where I was now.

In the distance, a tug hooted at a phosphate ship, whose deep throat hummed in return. My eyes turned to the sounds.

A quarter mile away, beyond the last remnant of this abandoned basin, beyond the spot where the police had watched, and beyond the end of the crumbling roadway, dark glassless windows stared back at me from the hollow carcass of the circus train.

Suddenly I yearned for the Colt .45 Peacemaker nestled in its box at home.

I began to move slowly toward the train. Weeds in bloom sagged over the broken sidewalk after I passed the last shielding building. Exposed on all sides, I stepped carefully over litter and made my way around jagged chunks of concrete. Out here the smell of the sea was fresh.

A brown rabbit darted across the damp field of coral and I wondered what kept its feet from being cut to ribbons in this grotesque environment. A pile of barnacle-encrusted blue crab traps loomed to the right. They, too, were decaying. Stepping over a long-fallen utility pole, I brushed a fat kingsnake. Its blood cooled almost to the point of coagulation, it crawled sluggishly away, skirting the standing water. At about half the distance between the train and the bakery, I left the sidewalk, or what was left of it, and, avoiding tangles of nettles, angled toward the western end of the weather-beaten train. A barn owl flew across my path in slow, purposeful flight, checking me out for nutritional value. A pair of fruit bats followed soon after, noisy, nervous, interested not the slightest in me. Wading through the vegetation, I reached the nearest tracks and felt the uncertain shifting of rock ballast beneath me. Moonlight reflected dimly from fat globules of resin oozing out of crossties.

As I crossed the last track, I peered down the line of gray, hump-backed cars with the faded legend on their sides: Rudyard E. Strong Shows—the Midway of Thrills. Marlinsport, Florida, U.S.A. Here was the end of the dream. Two dozen railway cars forgotten on a forgotten siding.

I stood beside the last coach, a once elegant observation car with a rear platform where the circus owner could stretch out in splendor and watch the denuded towns slip into history. Grasping the pitted hand bar, I hoisted myself to the high first step. The message on an enamel plate centered on the rear grillwork was destroyed, eaten by rust. I swept away a few cobwebs and pushed my way through a sagging door. Inside, through gashed and ragged windows, soft moonlight poured like silver smoke. The floor sagged and squealed under my weight as I walked slowly through the musty car. Comfort didn't seem to have mattered much to the circus owner. The car was less than utilitarian; it was severe. Bedsteads—the mattresses long gone—were one-by-three boards over storage bins. An old poster, dating from the 1940s, hung from a lone tack. Walled off with cheap boards, the toilet was simply a hole over the tracks.

I stopped. There were no sounds. At the other end of the car I pushed into the vestibule. Here, too, cheapness was the rule. There were no bellows covering the sides to protect the circus hands as they moved from car to car, merely a steel plate spanning the gap where the couplers met. The next car was like the first.

I moved stealthily in the dark, but doors still scraped and floor plates squeaked. Even so, I didn't want to pinpoint my presence with the flashlight. I thought about the deadline for tomorrow's *Trib*. It was going to come and go before I got back in touch with the desk. I wondered how Wilson would like it if I told him the truth—that I was pursuing the solution to two murders and our missing publisher by reliving my first big story, and failure. At the fourth coach I glanced out the windows on my left and received a jolt. Outside was a toolshed with a broken roofline, grown up with weeds and palmettos. Between the shed and the circus train, hidden from view on all sides, was a battered old Chevrolet sedan. Owen Blair's car.

So quietly I could not tell myself when they touched the floor, I pulled off my shoes. Each step now took cunning. I moved forward, checking outside right and left for eyes looking back at me. It took maybe ten minutes to inch open the door and slide silently through the fifth car. The Chevy was behind me now. If my search of the train turned up nothing I would circle back and check it out.

The doors between the fifth and sixth cars were jammed open. A faint smell from the nearest car's toilet told why. I tiptoed past the privy and across the open vestibule. Blair might be using this car for his base. I stood very still and listened. Could he have seen me already? The only sound was the faraway hoot of an owl. I crept forward. The sixth car's passageway was unlike the others. It jogged to the left and ran for twenty-five feet or so beside compartments before cutting back. I moved up apprehensively to each narrow doorway. All were open, and empty. I moved as noiselessly as morning mist around the last turn. In the moonlight, I squinted to make out the huddled form in the dark corner some fifteen feet away from me. It was Walter Hammersmith, propped up on the floor against a small table, his hands bound behind him and a gag in his mouth. His feet, somewhat askew but bound, rested against a narrow locker on the other side. He stared toward me with steady, unblinking eyes.

I approached him slowly.

"Owen?" I mouthed silently as I came near. His head rolled no, tentatively, then nodded yes. Utter bewilderment was in his eyes.

I knelt beside him and began to work on the gag. It was a sock tied in with another wrapped around his face. Once the gag was off, he leaned forward coughing and blowing out lint. His mouth must have been dry as death. I went to work on his hands.

"Where's Owen?" I whispered urgently as the ropes fell away.

There was no answer, but his hand fell to my wrist and

193

squeezed a warning. I saw the dark stain spotting his shirt-sleeve. His left hand was gashed and still moist with blood.

"Are you okay?" I whispered into his ear.

He struggled to speak. Then I saw a grimace of horror cross his face.

Wind whistled through the vestibule door behind me and I heard the words, "So long, String Bean."

There was no time to react. A haze of shock drowned me. A razor-sharp knife had stabbed at my shoulder blade and slid downward until it was stopped by the leather belt at my trousers. It stung more than hurt, but the smell and warmth and stickiness of my blood sent waves through my body. Strength drained from me like water through a broken dam.

Owen jumped to face me and crouched in the classic pose of the knife-fighter. He gauged my condition as I sagged against the wall and began slipping down it, leaving a wide red smear against the grimy surface.

"Slow you down, String Bean?"

"Holy Christ," I muttered. Numbness and pain alternated. Owen gave me a bad-toothed grin, still keeping his distance, tossing the long knife from hand to hand. I shifted feebly, sitting in a pool of my own blood.

"You should have stayed skinny, String Bean." He danced toward me and away. "I wouldn't have had to cut you so bad if you weren't such a horse."

"Good God," Hammersmith begged, "let me staunch his bleeding."

"Shut up," Blair retorted. "He shouldn't have come messing in my business."

"But for the . . ."

"You want me to open your belly like I did the cop's?"

Blair was grim-faced as he straightened from a crouch.

"No, please."

"All right. Then let's get back to this." He picked up a scrapbook from the table and stabbed at a passage with the point of his knife. "This says the ransom money was carried by Delano inside Mendez Bakery in my duffel bag, which looked like an old-time bolita pouch."

Even drifting toward unconsciousness, I recognized the words of my twenty-year-old kidnapping story and realized through the fog that this was the source of Delano's hate for me. A description of a bag, meant as an apt image befitting our town at that time, had been taken by Delano as a deliberate reminder by me of the scandal at the Casino. A moan rolled from my tight lips. If he'd only known how green I was, how ignorant I was of his past.

". . . honchos in this burg set me up," Blair's voice penetrated my wanderings. ". . . all those years in prison for a lousy twenty-five grand . . . Delano wouldn't tell me . . . the fucker . . . now you better talk."

Walter's voice was raw and shaky. "If Delano took it in the dark bakery, he died with the secret. There's no way I could know, for God's sake. It could even be the cops who picked you up helped themselves to a packet or two."

"Why did that fuckin' editor come see me?" Blair demanded angrily, his voice coming to me as if from another room. I felt myself slipping down on the floor. "He knew something, the bastard."

A cry of anguish spilled from Walter. "Palmer's dying."

"Shut up about him," Owen snarled, but I sensed more than saw his turning to me. Bending slightly, he stared at me from under those dark brows. My eyes were glazing as I watched his chest rise and fall rapidly. He inched closer, peering at me, his blade inches from my chest.

195

My eyelids started to flutter.

"Hey, String Bean, I'm sorry you ended like this." Leaning forward, he reached out with his free hand to feel my heart.

It was a terrible mistake. My left hand sprang to his throat and closed around it so tightly and so quickly he was caught with empty lungs. But that wasn't his only problem. I was crushing his larynx.

I barely heard Walter's cry of surprise. Although my right hand was there to fend it off, the knife was not a threat. It dangled from Blair's hand. He no longer wanted to stab me. All he wanted was air and an end to the pain that was exploding in his brain. His eyes turned beet red. I held on, willing strength into my fingers. I couldn't tell if the heart I heard pounding in the moonlight-drenched room was Owen's or my own.

"My God, my God!" Walter groaned.

The knife tumbled to the floor and Owen desperately wrestled with my fingers, clawing and tugging. I brought up my right hand and doubled my grip. No sound escaped Blair's lips. It was impossible. Finally his hands only fluttered against my wrist. Then they fell limply to the floor of the railway coach. I released him. His body collapsed.

Walter dropped to his knees beside me. "I'll get you to a hospital."

"No." I struggled to remain conscious. "I can't walk and you can't carry me . . . Get his keys."

His tortured eyebrows showed his loathing for the idea of touching Blair's body, but a sideways look at me spurred him on. He fumbled through Owen's pockets and pulled out a key ring.

"Go," I urged him. "Get help. Hurry."

Walter swallowed hard. His caterpillar brows spread in

stress as he got to his feet and started for the door on shaky legs. There he hesitated, looked back at Owen Blair and me.

"Hurry. Or there'll be two dead men for the police."

"You saved my life tonight," Walter said, and clattered down the steps of the train. In moments I heard the Chevy rumble to life.

A faint sighing noise came from Blair. With a great effort I rolled him face up. My shirt pulled loose from the floor as I leaned forward. Nausea whirled through me. My hands trembling, I picked up Owen Blair's bloody knife and placed the point against his throat.

Then I pushed.

TWENTY-SIX

The room was cool, pale green, and quiet. I was lying on my side in a hard, too small bed, my feet pushed against a metal bar. They'd brought me to St. Vincent's, thank goodness. Marlinsport General has a lot more experience with cuts but—maybe because of that—their stitching of wounds looks like butcher's string closing up a turkey carcass. St. Vincent's doctors have smaller fingers. Or something.

They'd told me it took hours to zip me back together and that I came near to pumping their blood bank dry. But except for a glucose IV, it was all behind me now. I was feeling pretty good, although, lying on my side, was getting old very fast.

My back didn't hurt in detail. If I'd felt every stitch it might have been worse than the overall burning and throbbing.

It was Saturday morning. Somehow I'd missed Friday.

Salgado was hangdogging it around my bed. He stationed himself beside me, fussing with the call button-on-acord like he'd never seen one before.

"You know how dumb that was, don't you? Going in after an armed man by yourself. That's our kind of work. Not yours."

"I'm sorry, Emilio. I didn't really believe he'd be there."

"It's just . . . damn it, that's why we carry guns, man!" He sounded hurt. "What kind of police force lets simple citizens chase down murderers?"

"How simple do you think I am?"

"Don't start joking. You have the worst timing for jokes of anybody I know."

"The cut's not so bad," I said.

"Tell me all about it. Your back looks like the railroad track from Pensacola to Key West."

My laugh quickly turned into a groan. "Now who's trying bad jokes?" I muttered.

"Sorry. It wasn't meant as a joke. Mere graphic illustration. Something a mule might understand."

"I'm working on it."

His eyes appraised my room. Sunshine coming in the window was hardening from soft warmth to summertime hot.

"Sure you're up to talking to me?" he asked.

"Yeah. How's Blair?"

"It's going to take a lot of trouble and tax money to get him ready for the electric chair." He smiled. "The surgeon threatened to sue you for malpractice when he saw your slaughterhouse tracheotomy."

"I knew I was botching it."

He leaned forward and rested his hand on my shoulder. "It was a mess. And the only thing in the world that could have saved him."

"Owen Blair's whole life has been a rat hole."

"Hah. Don't get philosophical about him. He's a cop killer and will ride Old Sparky for sure."

"I'd like to see him."

"I imagine you'd like to see the Dalai Lama, too."

"What does that mean?"

"Means you're not going to."

"Where is he?"

"I don't know. Tibet somewhere."

"I mean Owen, damn it."

"I don't think he's in Tibet."

"I see. He's in the prison ward at Marlinsport General."

"Get that look off your face. Do you have any idea the mess I'd be in with the state attorney if I let a witness interview the accused before trial?"

"I only want to ask him a couple of questions."

"He's not in any shape to talk to anyone. Won't be for a long time."

"Is he conscious?"

"Forget it. Blair won't be using his voice box for weeks. Maybe months. Ask me your questions."

I stared at him a long time. "Okay. Here's one for you. What'd you find on the circus train?"

"Enough to convict him on an array of charges, including the attempted murder of A.J. There were makings for more bombs of prison napalm. What do you think of that?"

"The nasty son of a bitch. I'm not surprised. What else?"

"Number one, his right shoe matched the bloody print at Delano's house. We also retrieved the scrapbooks, the knife that killed Delano, which was the same one used on you, and by you, Archie Lameroux's notebook, plus papers and ID scattered around from Walter Hammersmith's wallet."

"You found the notebook." I tried to sit up. It was a particularly bad idea.

"Yeah. It was filled with lots of symbols and cramped writing but no real information. On the day he died there were several notations about Delano beside your name."

"That's right," I said. "How about the scrapbooks? What was in them?"

"What you suspected. Years of police stories going all the way back to the Casino raid where Delano believed to his dying day he was entrapped. One book included every inconsequential story you ever wrote. When this is over, I'll give it to you. Nobody else could possibly want it."

"And the kidnapping?"

"Half of one book was devoted to it. And I'd say from the recent food stains and comments written over the stories that Blair pored over and over them."

"What did he write?"

Salgado laughed. "He had a limited vocabulary. 'Lying bastards' and 'shitheads.' He particularly didn't like one of Lameroux's editorials and messed it up in a disgusting way. Of course, it will be used in evidence."

"Anything else?"

"Well, he did make a notation on one story that Chastain was surrounded by dogs and he wrote one word across the picture of the bank president who provided part of the ransom—dead."

"So that's why he went after Hammersmith."

"Yeah. Seems like he wanted revenge against anyone who had a role in putting him away."

Salgado checked his watch and stood. "The doctor told the others I'm your last visitor for a while. Get some rest." He laid the call button carefully beside my pillow.

I must have dozed, for sometime in the afternoon food carts in the hall startled me. I opened my eyes and saw that the rays of sunlight pouring in through the window were long and hazy. A blur in the middle of the window ledge, covered with books and boxes of booze, gradually came into focus. It was a vase of flowers. White daisies. I reached painfully for the card. For the first time that day I felt a real smile tug at my cracked lips. Only A.J. would think to bring the fallen giant flowers.

TWENTY-SEVEN

Laughter crowded the great room. The voices of *Tribune* staffers old and young gloated in a triumph over the New Seville *Times*. I had to give it to Wilson. He'd proved himself a master of organization. Although it was Sunday, he'd had the beer and booze trucked in along with two portable bars. And the spread of food was lavish. The caterer must have been boiling shrimp and washing strawberries for hours.

Wilson had prodded me to let him host a party for me at my own house. "It's another Pulitzer for certain. A fucking Pulitzer Prize! It's the story of the decade."

My efforts to stall were greeted with derision. How could Palmer Kingston turn down a party? So Wilson had his way. It was almost as rough on A.J. as on me. She was doing her best to ignore shocked looks from a few *Trib* reporters who knew her and nasty anti-*Times* cracks from those who didn't. When Wilson finally realized who she was, he tried to hire her on the spot and either failed to notice or refused to acknowledge her look of disdain.

Smiling tightly, I stood with my back to the wall. Through my shirt I felt the faint comforting warmth of my neon flamingo. It was unlikely any overstoked friend could reach me here with a brotherly squeeze or an affectionate pat on the back. The crowd spilled out around the pool, but I knew the rumbling of distant thunder meant they would soon come crushing in. Flashes of lightning illuminated the stained-glass clerestory windows overhead. Paula, in something gold with a deep-cut bodice, was dancing vigorously with first one partner, then another. Always she seemed to be only a step or two away, and her eyes were on me. I was glad she could be so happy. I hoped my smile was not as wooden and insincere as it felt.

Above the music I could hear rain beginning to slash at the high windows. In a burst of squeals and laughter, the people outside ran indoors, sloshing drinks. As the rain intensified, the band got hotter and hotter. *Tribune* people were partying tonight on a level I hadn't seen in many years. I thought soberly that it would be a benchmark for them.

A scattering of applause erupted by the main door. I peered over the heads of those around me and had my grimmest expectation fulfilled. Walter Hammersmith was shedding his dripping wet raincoat. He nodded to right and left, acknowledging greetings from employees he did not know by name, or sight, or reputation. At a few— Moses, Paula, and Wilson—some light of recognition came to his dark, tangle-browed visage. But this was brief. For most of the others, this was a case of a giant of the *Tribune* made flesh.

His appearance at the party set the blood pulsing through my wound like a drumbeat. As he parted the crowd on his way to me, I remembered him poised in the corroded doorway of that railroad car and looking back for a moment before flying for help—before saving my life as I had saved his.

"You shouldn't be here," I said. My voice was low.

"I wanted to come," he said, extending his hand to me, "to thank you publicly."

My gaze roamed over to where A.J. was watching us from the kitchen door. I ignored the outstretched hand.

"Walter, we need to talk."

"Okay, but I want a drink. After all, this is a party. Which way's the bar?"

I pointed across the room. "When you get your drink, join me in the library through those double doors over there." I faked a smile at Paula and made my way carefully along the wall.

Randy Holliman had a long-stemmed copygirl backed against a leather love seat when I came stiffly through the door. A look at me and they scooted off to another room. I drew the doors behind Walter as he came in carrying two martinis. I refused the one offered to me and he settled onto the love seat Randy had envisioned as home plate.

"This house is obscene, Palmer. Take all those old signs out of that big room and you could pass for Spanish royalty. You're a one-suit reporter who had the dumbfounding good fortune to marry a smart woman."

"You'll get no argument from me on that."

I took a deep breath. My back was to the library doors. The skin across my stitches tightened.

He was hunched forward, almost like Delano in his chair. His red hands, one bandaged, kept playing with the martinis, moving first one glass behind the other, then repeating. His eyes focused on the thick clarity of the gin.

"What the hell's wrong with you?" he growled.

The hind glass slid wetly around the other. A little jostle of gin spattered on the tabletop. His eyes did not meet mine. He was guessing what was wrong.

Behind me the door rattled as someone tried to come in. I held the handles behind my back until he or she gave up.

"I'll tell you what's wrong."

Walter gulped at a martini.

"Archie Lameroux knew you skimmed part of the ransom money, didn't he?"

The eyes peered up, as cold as gin from the freezer. "Watch it. I'm getting angry."

"I'm outraged!" I shouted.

Those two words were to live in *Tribune* lore. Outside in the big room everybody heard them—or later said they did.

"Now wait," Walter demanded. "What did Archie tell you? He . . . the man was almost senile. You can't put trust in the maundering . . ."

"Shut up, Walter."

"Damn, man. I saved your life!"

The handles rattled again. I locked the door and crossed to the mantel. Walter was sagging over my coffee table. He looked like Delano's ghost.

"Jesus, Walter, I figured that would be your last line of defense, not your first. What happened to 'I didn't do it'?"

"An addled old man spun a conspiracy theory for a naive disciple. I need no defense to that."

"Archie Lameroux spun no theory. I'm on my own here."

The beetling brows reacted with quick surprise. "He didn't feed you this?"

"No."

Something at the core of the man seemed to relax. His eyes still gleamed, but something in my one-word denial was like a healing medicine to him. Still, he looked puzzled.

"You're one of the most careful reporters in the business. What possible evidence do you have to back up so preposterous a charge?"

"I have no evidence."

"And you dare accuse me of . . . of . . ."

"Of theft. Certainly insider trading. Probably tax evasion. And murder."

The last word brought him to his feet. He was so startled he couldn't speak for a moment. His eyes went to the doors, then at the arched windows leading to the pool, and then back at me, leaning miserably against the mantel and hating every moment of this interview.

"You admit there is no evidence yet you dare accuse me of a thing like that? You left your sickbed too soon."

"I cannot prove that you stole from the ransom funds or wrote down false serial numbers so that the money couldn't be traced, but I believe it is so."

"Slanderous supposition!" There was malice in his eyes now, and a jaw you ordinarily didn't notice. "Even allowing for your pathetic mental state I can't see how a reporter of your background could make such reckless accusations."

"You stole the twenty-five thousand dollars and I know what you did with it. In a way, Archie Lameroux did help me with that. A tape recording he made at the prison with Owen Blair was wrapped in a scrap of an old *Tribune* . . . from the classifieds . . . an ad for trucks."

"Trucks? What in God's name do trucks have to do with me?"

"That's what Lameroux could never prove, even if he was on the right track. The ad and tape tell me that much.

The trail led only to Artie Brent, not to you, and we all know in what contempt you hold him, right? Except Artie's told me he fronts for all sorts of people in Marlinsport, people who don't want their names attached to particular enterprises."

Walter stood frozen. He wanted me to think he was appalled by the unjustness of what I was saying. But there was fear in his voice.

"Wilson would throw your ass out in the street if you turned in a story with nothing more than this behind it. As the *Tribune*'s publisher, I honestly don't see how I can justify keeping so reckless an individual on the staff."

"Somewhere, in Tallahassee or in Artie's records, I'll find how you own Jones Trucking. And then a look at your tax returns will show if you bothered to pay taxes on all that extra income."

"You can forget that. Tax records don't go back twenty years. You still have nothing."

I shrugged. A twinge in my back made me wish I hadn't.

"I will get enough to show why you killed Archie Lameroux."

Walter was pacing before my books. "I'm not going to take this shit from you, Palmer. I'm leaving."

"Not until we deal with Archie Lameroux," I said sharply. "You saw me talking to him last Saturday. Next thing you know Wilson's shaking the money tree to fly me to Chicago to find Owen Blair. You scotched that, but it preyed on your mind, didn't it?"

"I could get you committed on the basis of this conversation, but the scandal would ruin the *Tribune*."

"Don't talk *Trib* to me. You killed the best thing about it."

His face drained of color. "Palmer. Believe me. I beseech you. This is madness."

I spoke slowly. "Now we come to the place where evidence will be abundant."

There was half a martini left. Walter picked it up and moved to the windows and watched the gray rain pound across the patio. Methodically he crushed the olive as I watched.

"Proof of murder? Impossible."

"I've been aboard the *Mil Line Rater*."

"Damn you! You had no right to go snooping around my boat."

"It's clear enough that's where you killed Lameroux. Remember, I've been a crime reporter for a long, long time and I'm telling you there's no way you've cleaned all the blood out of that carpet. Clubbing a man to death with a fire extinguisher must have been a messy business."

The martini glass fell to the floor. I swallowed hard, searching the face of the man I'd worked for all those years.

"You were scared, weren't you, Walter, that he'd tell me his suspicions? Well, he didn't tell me a damn thing. You killed him for nothing."

There was a cold silence in the room. The sounds of the band and the echoing laughter came from a different world. I realized that my back was throbbing. I released my grip on the mantel.

"This is crazy," Walter's voice broke. "I could never kill Archie."

"I wish that were so, more than you can possibly know. But it's not. When Salgado told me about finding Lameroux's notebook on the circus train, the message was clear. If Owen Blair had killed Lameroux, he wouldn't have taken an appointment book and left behind a wallet with a hundred dollars. On the other hand, you were eager to know everything you could about Lameroux's thoughts and actions during the last days of his life. I'm afraid there were two killers on that circus train."

Walter's eyebrows settled, but still he stood there staring at the broken glass. At last he spoke. "I will listen to no more."

"Walter, I'm writing a story."

"You will hurt the *Tribune*."

"I know."

"Have you told anyone?"

"Not yet."

He smiled and slowly sank back on the couch. "Can't bear to destroy the celebration in there?"

"I had to talk to you first. Fairness and all."

"Fairness and all," he repeated, more to himself. "Say that I deny everything. That will be sufficient."

"Come with me to talk to Salgado. It has to be done."

His eyes met mine then. A fury was working on him, and he was fighting for control.

"By the time the *Tribune* lawyers go over your wild tale and see how much is speculation and how little is fact, you won't have enough copy for a short on the local page."

"I'd guess a plaster cast of the damage to Lameroux's skull will exactly match the type of small fire extinguisher you're missing. And you have no alibi."

"Alibi? You dare use that word in connection with me? I can destroy you."

But he was still sitting down. As his gaze traveled up to meet mine, our relative positions came home to him. "You've told Salgado nothing yet?"

"You're not listening to me."

"You've told him nothing?"

"That's right."

"Well, thanks for that," he said.

I stared at him. "I just don't understand. You'd gotten away with it for twenty years. All Lameroux had were old suspicions. Why did you kill him?"

"I admit nothing." He looked steadily at me for a long time. "Don't you realize that old and impotent as he was, Archie Lameroux could still pose a tremendous threat."

"How?"

"He had you. You may be a two-bit reporter but you're the best two-bit reporter around. And you worshipped him. You'd hunt for a month on a single word from Archie. So . . . if everything you guessed were true, Archie Lameroux died because of you."

When he arose and walked to the outside doors, I made no move to stop him. It was a long time before I could make myself rejoin the party.

TWENTY-EIGHT

The fan made its slow electric sound. I lay facedown on my disheveled, wadded-up bedclothes.

A.J. knelt on the floor beside the bed, her face next to mine.

"You're crying," she said, "but it isn't your back, is it?"

I couldn't move, or talk.

"I wish I could help," she whispered.

As the first gray light of dawn appeared in the window, A.J. stroked my hair and talked softly to me. Her presence dulled the pain of the night, but I knew from experience that a shadow of it would be with me always. She whispered about the party, trying to cheer me, at the same time not understanding why I was so sad. There was nothing I could tell her, not yet.

Her beeper and my telephone sounded almost at the same moment. We exchanged glances. Groaning, I eased my body off the bed.

A windy dawn found tiny breakers lapping at the side

of the police launch. Salgado, huddled in the stern, nursed a cup of coffee. A.J. and I stood apart. The smell of burnt petroleum poisoned the air as we reached our destination. Bits and pieces of scorched planking drifted past. None of us spoke. All we could do was stare down into the churning water at the dark shadow. The sun was climbing slowly above a cypress head to the east of the police boat.

A diver surfaced. He pulled off his mask and yelled. "That's a big sucker down there, Chief. Burned to the water line and capsized."

"Is it the *Mil Line Rater?*"

"Yep. I guess the report was right."

"Any sign of a body?"

"No, but there's a strong current."

To the north inching toward us was a large floating crane. "We'll have it righted and refloated today," Salgado said. "This is about the place Jack Betancourt said Lameroux's body was dumped, isn't it, Palmer?"

I nodded.

"Yesterday you said you wanted to talk to me soon. Does this tie in with that?"

I peered down into the green bay. I could barely make out the encrusted hull of Walter Hammersmith's boat as it wallowed like a dead whale beneath the choppy water. I could feel A.J.'s eyes on me.

"Probably. We still need to talk," I said, and looking at A.J., added, "later."

"Okay, but you should know Hammersmith was last seen by the guard at the Yacht Club late last night. If he was on this thing there's no way he could have survived such a fire. I'm afraid your publisher is dead."

I went to the back of the police boat and carefully sat down. It was the beginning of a very hard day.

The next morning A.J. and I awaited high tide at the Banana Docks. Staring out into the gray haze, we sat side by side on the front seat of the Packard. The gear shift protruded from the floor between us like a sentry. Beyond the heavy chrome hood ornament, my eyes were focused on a dark mass in the channel. It moved slowly toward us on the incoming tide.

"It was a remarkable story, Palmer. I've never read another like it. You made the case against Walter Hammersmith without ever coming out and saying he killed your editor."

"The story should have been stronger. If I'd done it a day earlier or if I'd told Salgado what was in my mind . . . Thin as it was I had to threaten to resign and give it to you guys before Wilson agreed to let it run."

"How did you get on to Hammersmith in the first place?"

I slapped my hand aganst the steering wheel. "It was the Packard. A simple dented fender that was half my fault and suddenly Jones started throwing money at me. When I realized how well Artie Brent knew his way around Walter's boat I knew their often-stated dislike for each other was just a pose. In fact it was Artie who unwittingly revealed that Walter never made it to the university dinner. And when I spotted a black bowtie on the boat, well, I figured out what had happened. Walter picked up Lameroux and took him out for a ride."

"Have you talked to Artie about Hammersmith's death?"

"No, although I've tried."

The patch in the rain-speckled channel had halved the distance to us.

"That's seaweed, Palmer."

"Probably."

"Even if it is him, what are you going to do? This feels creepy."

"Cover him with a blanket I've got in the trunk. I can't stand to think of them uncovered."

"It's hyacinths." She turned to me. "Where is Hammersmith, at the bottom of the bay or in Rio?"

The hyacinths clustered around the piling under the pier. The delicate lavender flowers floated in a soup of litter and garbage. I started the engine of my battered Packard and limped slowly off the dock.

"My guess is Rio."

THE MEASURE OF A MAN
IS HOW WELL HE SURVIVES LIFE'S

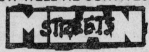

BOLD NEW CRIME NOVELS BY
TODAY'S HOTTEST TALENTS

BAD GUYS
Eugene Izzi
_____ 91493-8 $3.95 U.S.   _____ 91494-6 $4.95 Can.

CAJUN NIGHTS
D.J. Donaldson
_____ 91610-8 $3.95 U.S.   _____ 91611-6 $4.95 Can.

MICHIGAN ROLL
Tom Kakonis
_____ 91684-1 $3.95 U.S.   _____ 91686-8 $4.95 Can.

SUDDEN ICE
Jim Leeke
_____ 91620-5 $3.95 U.S.   _____ 91621-3 $4.95 Can.

DROP-OFF
Ken Grissom
_____ 91616-7 $3.95 U.S.   _____ 91617-5 $4.95 Can.

A CALL FROM L.A.
Arthur Hansl
_____ 91618-3 $3.95 U.S.   _____ 91619-1 $4.95 Can.

TOUGH STREETS

The grit, the dirt, the cheap cost of life—the ongoing struggle between the law...and the lawbreakers.

BIG TIME TOMMY SLOANE
James Reardon
_____ 90981-0 $3.95 U.S.   _____ 90982-9 $4.95 Can.

TIGHT CASE
Edward J. Hogan
_____ 91142-4 $3.95 U.S.   _____ 91143-2 $4.95 Can.

RIDE A TIGER
Harold Livingston
_____ 90487-8 $4.95 U.S.   _____ 90488-6 $5.95 Can.

THE RIGHT TO REMAIN SILENT
Charles Brandt
_____ 91381-8 $3.95 U.S.   _____ 91382-6 $4.95 Can.

THE EIGHTH VICTIM
Eugene Izzi
_____ 91218-8 $3.95 U.S.   _____ 91219-6 $4.95 Can

THE TAKE
Eugene Izzi
_____ 91120-3 $3.50 U.S.   _____ 91121-1 $4.50 Can.